Elizabeth Laird was born in New Zealand but when she was two the family moved to England. Since then she has travelled to the furthest corners of the world and has encountered all kinds of animals. On one adventure she became lost at night in a Kenyan game reserve, coming a little too close to an angry rhino and narrowly avoiding buffalo and elephants. Her experience of the wild animals of Africa has helped her write the *Wild Things* series.

She is the award-winning author of *Red Sky in the Morning*, *Kiss the Dust*, *Secret Friends* (shortlisted for the 1997 Carnegie Medal) and many other children's novels.

Elizabeth Laird has been helped in her research for *Wild Things* by wildlife experts and local people in Kenya, whose lives are constantly touched by the animals amongst which they live.

Books available in the Wild Things series

1. Leopard Trail
2. Baboon Rock
3. Elephant Thunder
4. Rhino Fire
5. Red Wolf

Coming soon

6. Zebra Storm   December 1999

All Wild Things titles can be ordered at your
local bookshop or are available by post from
Book Service by Post (tel: 01624 675137).

WILD THINGS

RED WOLF

Elizabeth Laird

MACMILLAN CHILDREN'S BOOKS

*Series consultant: Dr Shirley Strum
with the support of Dr David Western,
past director of the Kenya Wildlife Service*

First published 1999 by Macmillan Children's Books
a division of Macmillan Publishers Limited
25 Eccleston Place, London SW1W 9NF
Basingstoke and Oxford
www.macmillan.co.uk

Associated companies throughout the world

ISBN 0 330 37152 5

1 3 5 7 9 8 6 4 2

A CIP catalogue record for this book is available from
the British Library.

Phototypeset by Intype London Ltd
Printed and bound in Great Britain by Mackays of Chatham plc, Kent

For Yonas, Rahel and Hirut

whose father, Teklehaímanot Yigletu, is brilliant at spotting wolves. He drove me all the way up into the high mountains of Ethiopia to find them. We found Dr Karen Laurenson and Dr Claudio Sillero-Zubiri there too, and they welcomed me kindly to their remote research station where they study the wolves and try to protect them, and they shared with me their unique knowledge and great enthusiasm.

Macmillan Children's Books and Elizabeth Laird would like to thank Dr David Macdonald, Professor of Zoology at Oxford University, and the British Council in Ethiopia, who provided logistical support during Elizabeth Laird's research in the Bale Mountains in Ethiopia.

Flurries of snow had fallen in the night, and the wind had been bitterly cold. The wolves had woken early, chilled even through their thick fur. The sun was rising quickly now from behind the far hills, turning the mountain tops first a rosy pink and then a brilliant gold, and the wolves lifted their muzzles to the sky and howled out their morning song in long trills of falling sound.

The pack had slept in the open, huddled together for warmth, except for the mother and her litter of pups, who had spent the night in their den in a shallow cave below a low ridge of boulders.

The mother came out of it now, her russet back glowing red against the grey-green shrubs that grew close to the ground. Her darker pups tumbled out after her and at once began to play, falling over each other, rolling and biting, yapping and whining. One trotted to his mother and thrust his blunt nose under her belly to find a teat. The others followed, and soon all of them were drinking together.

After a moment, the mother wolf shook herself

free and walked over to the other adults of the pack who were nuzzling each other's faces in their ritual morning greeting.

The sun rose fast. Its intense African heat would melt the ice and snow long before mid-morning. Soon it would be too hot to hunt and the wolves would flop down onto the ground to rest. Now, though, it was time to be active.

The adults set off on their morning foray, patrolling and marking the borders of their territory. The mother watched them go. They would return soon, and one of them would stay to guard her pups while she went hunting. She would need to hunt well today if she was to satisfy their hunger.

She sat back on her haunches and looked out over her high, windswept world. Far below this remote mountain top was the heat and dust of Ethiopia. There were people there with their villages and towns, their cattle and dogs.

Miles away, a dog barked. The wolf turned her head, curious and watchful, and listened. The barking came again. Another dog joined in, and a chorus of snarling and growling floated up to her from far below.

Uneasily the mother turned back to her pups. She stood over them, every sense alert, scanning the horizon, while the fur lifted on her neck and a faint growl rumbled in her throat.

1

DRUMS IN THE DARK

A cock crowed raucously just outside the shut-tered window of the pilgrim's inn and Afra stirred in her sleep. She opened her eyes and stared, bemused, into the pitch dark. Where was she? Why was it so dark? And who was breathing on the other side of the room?

Then she remembered, and a shiver ran down her spine. She was in Ethiopia at last! And right outside the window, under the cold night sky, lay Lalibela, the ancient holy city in the heart of the mountains, where her mother, dead now for so many years, had been born. And it was Prof, her father, who was sleeping on the bed in the far corner.

She shivered again, with cold this time, then lay down and pulled the blanket up under her chin. Prof's breathing turned to gentle snores as he rolled over, but there wasn't a sound from Tom, in the third bed, next to hers. He must still be fast asleep.

She'd be asleep, too, if it wasn't for the knot that was tying and untying itself so strangely in her stomach. Yesterday had been exhausting.

They'd flown from Nairobi to Addis Ababa, and then had to wait hours for the little twelve-seater plane to Lalibela. The flight had been so bumpy that Tom had thrown up. She might have felt sick, too, if her mind hadn't been racing so fast.

Prof had hardly ever spoken to her about her mother, but on the few occasions when she'd dared to bring the subject up he'd always said the same thing.

'I told you, honey. Her family disappeared during the civil war. I mean, it was mayhem out there, all over Ethiopia. Her father died years ago, before I met your mother even, and her own mother wasn't exactly young. Her brother, her cousins – all of them – must either have gotten out of the country, escaping through the borders, making for Europe or the States maybe, or else they were killed. I wrote so many people, trying to find out, but I never had any answers. They just weren't around any more.' He'd taken her chin between his finger and thumb then, and gently pinched it. 'Don't build up any hopes, Afra. Accept it. Your mother's family has gone.'

Afra wriggled her head on the hard lumpy pillow, trying to find a comfortable position.

But he doesn't know for sure, she thought. Not totally, definitely, a hundred per cent. The people he wrote to – anything might have been going on with them. They could have been moving house when the letter came, or the mail didn't work

4

properly, or maybe they just didn't get around to answering, like I never get around to writing to Aunt Tidey. I bet – I just *know* – there's someone left, someone who knew her, some little piece of my family somewhere around here.

She'd been so sure that something would happen that she'd scanned the face of every Ethiopian they'd met yesterday, looking for clues, almost expecting someone to stop in their tracks when they caught sight of her and greet her by name.

A dull, deep, thrilling note suddenly reverberated through the small stone room, then another, and another, coming now in a regular slow rhythm.

It's a drum, thought Afra. Someone's beating a drum!

She wanted to know what time it was. It was much too dark to see her watch so she stretched out her hand to grope for the torch on the table by her bed. Her fingers met another hand, reaching towards her in the total darkness, and she gave a little scream. An answering gasp came from the bed on the far side of the table.

'It's only me,' said Tom. 'Who did you think it was? Count Dracula?'

He started making ghostly moans.

'Don't,' said Afra, shuddering. 'It's too spooky not seeing anything at all. And what's that weird drumming noise going on out there?'

Prof's snoring had stopped abruptly, and Afra heard a rustle as he pulled his arm out of his sleeping bag to look at the luminous dial on his watch.

'Half past five,' he said, his voice still thick with sleep. 'Why does everything start at dawn in this country?'

'What's starting? Do you mean the drums?' asked Tom, who sounded wide awake already.

'It's the service in the church,' said Prof. He gave a mighty yawn. 'Time to get up, I guess, if we're going to get down there before it's all over.'

'A service? Church?' said Tom doubtfully. 'But it's not even Sunday.'

He'd only been to church a few times and it hadn't been exactly fun.

There was a small scraping noise, and Afra knew that Prof was groping about on the stone floor for his glasses.

'No point in missing it now we're here,' he said. 'It's not every day you get to witness ceremonies that were ancient when Columbus sailed for America.'

Afra felt her skin tingle.

And maybe there, in the church, I'll see a face and I'll know it's something to do with her, she thought.

Prof had already peeled off his sleeping bag and groped his way to the window. He threw back the rough wooden shutter. There was no glass in the window and a blast of even colder air rushed into the room. A few stars still shone out, pale pinpricks of light in the black sky, but they were fading one by one as grey streaks spread up from the horizon.

Afra fumbled for her clothes at the bottom of her bed and quickly put them on. Tom had dressed in no time, and, moving fast to beat the cold, Prof was already pulling on his thick jacket.

There were a few moments of confusion while the three of them fumbled about in the dark, looking for their shoes and putting them on.

'Ready?' said Prof, pulling back the squeaky bolt on the old wooden door. 'Bring the flashlight. We're going to need it.'

Their room opened onto a simple courtyard and a flight of steps ran down to a lower yard where a big door led out into the street. The night watchman had been sleeping under a shelter, wrapped in a white cotton shawl, and he got up, grumbling, to unlock the door.

Out in the street, the air was fresh and cold and the drumming noise seemed louder. It rose up out of the ground, funnelled through the honeycomb of tunnels that connected the deep pits in which the mysterious ancient churches stood. It echoed through the lanes of the little town, coiling up the mountainside above and rolling down into the deep valley below, vibrating on the corrugated iron roofs which were beginning to shine dully in the gathering dawn.

Grey shapes were slipping out of the houses as people stepped into the lane to make their way to the church, and a hundred dogs seemed to be in full voice, competing with each other in frenzied barking.

Prof was walking on fast ahead, and Afra and Tom stumbled along over the rough stones as they tried to keep up with him.

'This is amazing,' said Tom, turning to grin at Afra. 'It's like something out of a film. One of those kind of lost world films, you know, where they'll find the secret tomb of a dead emperor, stuffed with treasure, and a long-lost princess who was walled up alive.'

Afra didn't answer. The throbbing drums, sounding louder and louder now, and the first pink flushes of the rising sun, and the worn stones of this old lane, were making her breathless with an almost painful anticipation. She didn't want to be distracted by thoughts of movies.

She shot a sideways glance at Tom. He looked his usual self, his thatch of hair still rumpled from when he'd been in bed, his cheerful face eager and friendly. For a moment she almost regretted begging Prof to invite him along too. Tom belonged too much to his family, to his mum and dad, and his kid sister and new baby brother. He was too English, too ordinary. He'd never had a beautiful Ethiopian mother who had died when he was born, or a brilliant and erratic archaeologist father, or a secret quest to find the remnants of his family.

'Hey, did you hear that?' Tom said suddenly, stopping and raising his head. 'That kind of howling noise? Do you reckon it might have been a wolf?'

'A wolf? You have wolves in your brain, Tom. I bet they're all howling around in there and making you go crazy. It's a hyena, dumbo, somewhere up there on the mountain top.'

Tom looked crestfallen.

'Yeah, I suppose you're right.'

Afra heard the disappointment in his voice and wished she hadn't been so sharp. Tom did have a quest after all. He'd been going on and on about it. He'd read that there were wolves in these mountains, the last few survivors of an ancient and dying race. He didn't give a stuff about all the churches and monasteries that Prof wanted to drag them off to. He only wanted to see a wolf.

Me too, actually, thought Afra. I'd give anything to see a wolf.

She stumbled and nearly fell and, looking down, saw that her shoelace was untied.

'Go on,' she said. 'I'll follow you.'

She crouched down to tie her lace but a faint sound made her turn her head. Had she imagined it? No, there it was again. A kind of weak, hesitant whine.

Then she saw it. Lying on its side, huddled against the wall, was a puppy, his pale flanks heaving as he breathed.

Afra put out her hand and the puppy pulled back his lips in a pathetically defiant snarl.

'Why, you're all alone, little guy,' said Afra.

'Afra!'

She looked up. The tall figure of Prof, topped with his tousle of wild hair, stood silhouetted at the end of the lane. He sounded impatient.

'Take care now, I'll be back,' said Afra, and she ran on to catch the others up.

2

AFRA'S QUEST

The sky was lightening minute by minute as the sun rose. Prof had entered a deep rocky cleft, with Afra and Tom hurrying after him. He stopped at the black mouth of a tunnel and turned round.

'Do you have the flashlight?' he said.

Tom handed it to him.

'You mean we're going in there?' said Afra breathlessly.

The drum beat was confusing her. It was overlaid now with the sound of high chanting.

Prof switched the torch on and shone it into the mouth of the tunnel.

'Of course we are. Not far now.'

'Not far to where?' said Tom.

'To the church of Medhane Alem. The great church. Hear that drum? It's the beating heart of Lalibela.' He stepped into the tunnel and his voice echoed as he called back to them over his shoulder, 'Be careful where you put your feet. The floor's uneven in places.'

The torch beam wavered on the rough rock of the tunnel floor. Afra put her hands out to touch both sides as she felt her way along. The tunnel ended abruptly. She stepped out after the others and looked up wonderingly.

They were standing in a deep pit. Solid rock, cut straight and true, soared up all around them. The vast block of stone in the centre of the pit, which was the size of a huge building, had been sculpted to create a beautiful church, with pillars and windows and a flight of steps leading up to a door.

They went up the steps. There was a pile of shoes outside the door and Prof bent down and began to take off his own.

'What are you doing?' said Afra. 'They're not muddy.'

'You take them off in holy places here,' said Prof. 'To show respect.'

Afra and Tom kicked their shoes off too and followed Prof in through the door.

It had been growing brighter outside, but not much light penetrated this great, cavernous, living sculpture. A few tapers and candles cast a warm glow, and Afra followed with her eyes the bands of light as they flickered up the perfectly shaped pillars into the high carved vaults of the roof overhead.

In the centre of the church, sitting cross-legged on a rug on the floor, sat the white-robed drummers, and beside them was a boy, no older than Afra. He looked up momentarily from the book he was holding and met her eyes through the cloud of incense that billowed up from the silver vessel in front of him. His brown face glowed a coppery red in the light of the taper he held.

Afra felt a shock of recognition. There was something of herself in him and something, too, of the precious photograph of her mother which hung over her bed at home. She was used to the way people looked in Kenya, where she'd always lived. Sarah, who had more or less brought her up, and her foster brother Joseph were the people she knew best in the whole world. But they didn't look anything like her.

It was different here. The Ethiopians probably didn't think she looked like them at all. She was half white, half American, after all, but she felt a strange familiarity, a kind of kinship, a deep sort of knowledge that she couldn't explain even to herself.

This is the place. This is where I'm from, the real me, she thought, feeling with her toes the gently undulating surface of the hand-hewn floor which had been polished smooth by seven centuries of bare feet.

The boy, who was draped in a thick white shawl-like *shamma*, got to his feet and went to a kind of stand which held a heavy book the size of a large paving stone. The priest standing beside it handed him a taper, and the boy began to read, chanting words in a hoarse, rasping voice, rocking a little as he did so.

The words were strange and mesmerizing. Afra's eyes were fixed on the taper. She sensed around her the other worshippers who stood in the shadows with their backs to the walls. The air, except for the coiling incense smoke, was still. The boy's voice echoed from the vaults and pillars.

She turned and clutched at her father's sleeve. She thought she was going to faint.

'Prof,' she whispered. 'I'm going to pass out.'

His arm was around her at once and he guided her out through the door. She was vaguely aware of Tom behind her, feeling for his shoes in the pile by the step.

'Sit down here, honey,' said Prof. 'Put your head down on your knees.'

The fresh air made her feel better almost at once. She sank down and buried her head in her lap. The prickling blackness ebbed away and she felt fine again.

'Wow, what a nerdy thing to do,' she said, looking up. 'Passing out, I mean.'

Prof ran his hand through his hair.

'I'm sorry, kids,' he said. 'Maybe it wasn't such a great idea, dragging you out to church on your first day here.'

Afra shook her head vehemently.

'No, I loved it. It was . . . incredible. I felt . . .'

She stopped. She couldn't tell anyone how she'd

felt in there. She hardly knew herself. She shook her head, clearing away the last trace of faintness.

'Maybe it's the altitude. I mean, it's so high here. Or I'm just hungry or something.'

'Hungry!' Prof hooked a hand under her elbow and pulled her to her feet. 'Of course! Breakfast. We all need breakfast. That all right by you, Tom?'

Tom had been standing a little awkwardly behind them, not sure what to do. Now he laughed.

'You bet. I could eat six fried eggs and a ton of bacon.'

'You won't get bacon here, but eggs are an excellent idea,' said Prof. 'Come on. Let's put our shoes on and go see what they can fix for us at the hotel.'

The sun was well up now, its first hot fingers penetrating the pit. The rock was no longer grey but a golden pink, and a shaft of orange light lit up the tunnel. They wouldn't need the torch now.

They were walking up the rocky cleft again when they saw a middle-aged man hurrying down towards them. They stepped aside to let him pass. He was wearing city clothes, well-pressed trousers and a leather jacket, and he was carrying a brief-case. The top of his bald brown head shone in the glancing light of the newly risen sun as if it had been polished.

The sun was in his eyes, and he had to screw

them up to look at them as he came past. His glance moved quickly over Afra and Tom, but a quick frown creased his forehead when he caught sight of Prof, and he slowed down, nearly stumbling over a stone.

Why's he staring? thought Afra, her senses quivering and alert at once.

The man stopped dead in his tracks.

'Richard?' he said, looking intently at Prof. 'Richard Tovey?'

Prof stared back for a moment, then he gave a bark of astonished delight.

'Giorgis! It can't be! What are you doing here? This is incredible! I didn't even recognize you!'

The man rubbed his bald head and laughed.

'I had hair last time you saw me.'

Prof had grabbed his hand and was pumping it with awkward enthusiasm.

'I've thought of you so often. I tried to write you. I didn't know if . . . I mean—' He stopped awkwardly.

'If I'd survived all the fighting and the revolutionary purges?' said Giorgis, grinning. 'Only just, my dear friend. I got away to the States. I'm there most of the time now. It's a long story.' He turned to look at Tom. 'Who's this? Your son?'

Afra stiffened, but Prof put his arm round her and pulled her forward.

'No, but this is my daughter, Afra. Tom's our friend.'

Giorgis looked at Afra and lifted his eyebrows. The wrinkles in his forehead ran right up into his shiny brown scalp.

'Your daughter?'

He was looking at Afra properly now, and she felt the knot tighten again inside her. He turned back to Prof.

'You married her, then? You married Sablay? The eyes are the same. It's incredible.'

Afra felt something burst inside her.

'You knew her?' she said, starting forward out of Prof's encircling arm.

Giorgis put his hands on her shoulders and looked down at her.

'Yes, I knew her. Not well. Her brother, Seyoum, he was my good friend.'

Afra gasped. Questions boiled up inside her. Her uncle Seyoum had always been a distant, mysterious name, mentioned briefly and very occasionally, each reference to be snapped up and held in her heart like secret treasure.

'Where is he now?' she said breathlessly. 'Is he in Ethiopia? Is he still—' It was her turn to stop in mid-sentence. She couldn't bear to ask if her uncle had died.

Giorgis shook his head regretfully.

'I don't know what happened to him. We lost touch years ago. He went to Germany, I think. I'm here myself only occasionally.' He looked at Prof. 'They've brought me back as a consultant archaeologist, to work on the new historical survey of Lalibela. I'm meeting one of the high priests this morning. I can tell you, Richard, these guys are hard to pin down. If I'm late, maybe he'll refuse to see me at all.' He paused. 'Come with me. Can you still speak Amharic? You used to be pretty good.'

Tom nudged Afra.

'What's Amharic?' he whispered.

'The Ethiopian language,' she whispered back.

She turned back to look shyly at Giorgis once again. To Tom he might look only like a short, rotund, bald and middle-aged Ethiopian, but to Afra he was a messenger, a bearer of mysteries.

Prof was shaking his head regretfully.

'Hey, I'd love to, you know I would, but I'm with the kids and they need their breakfast.'

'It's OK,' said Tom. 'We can go back and get breakfast on our own.'

Afra wanted to kick him. She hated it at the best of times when Prof went off with his archaeological colleagues. He entered another world and closed the door behind him. But this would be the worst ever. Prof wouldn't only go away himself, he'd be going off with someone who might have in his possession a clue to her quest. And they'd be leaving her behind!

'They don't speak English at the hotel,' she said irritably. 'We won't know what to ask for.'

Giorgis looked surprised.

'What? Where are you staying?'

'At the old pilgrim's inn,' said Prof defensively.

Giorgis burst out laughing.

'What? Hard beds, and no flush toilets, and shutters instead of windows? Richard, you don't change! Why don't you stay at one of the tourist hotels?'

'Not my style,' Prof said shortly. 'Listen, Giorgis—'

'No, no, let the kids go. They can order their breakfast in Amharic, and I promise, I promise that we'll come back in no more than one hour's time, OK?' He bent down to smile directly into Afra's eyes. 'What do you want for breakfast?'

Reassured in spite of herself, she felt her frown melt away. 'I don't know,' she said. 'Bread. Eggs. Tea.'

'OK, fine. Bread is *dabo*. Eggs is *inkolal*. Tea is *shai*. Got that?'

His eyes were so amused and his smile so friendly that she couldn't help smiling back.

'*Dabo. Inkolal. Shai*,' she repeated. 'Is that really Amharic? I'm going to learn it.'

Giorgis straightened up.

'I'll look forward to that,' he said. 'Welcome to Ethiopia, Sablay's daughter.'

Tom was frowning, his eyes practically crossed with concentration.

'*Dabo, inkolal, shai*. Come on, Afra, let's go, before we forget.'

Prof pressed her nose with his forefinger. She shook it off. She hated it when he treated her like a baby, especially when she was angry with him.

'One and a half hours,' he said. 'I promise.'

Tom and Afra walked up out of the cleft of rock and the brilliant full sunshine of early morning hit them at the top.

'I'll race you back,' said Tom. '*Dabo, inkolal, shai.*'

He took off and began tearing down the road towards the inn. Afra followed more slowly. She ran half-heartedly for a few metres, then she slowed to a walk. The glory of the morning had been splintered.

'One and a half hours! Are you kidding?' she muttered under her breath. 'One day you'll forget I even exist.'

She was passing the place where she'd stopped to tie her shoelace, and she suddenly remembered the puppy. The little hollow by the wall, where he'd been before, was empty now. He wasn't lying there any more.

He found his mom I suppose, thought Afra. Good for him.

A movement in the dust a little further on caught her eye. She ran on to look at it more closely.

The puppy hadn't found his mother. He had been struggling to climb up onto a stone that the sun had begun to warm, but he had fallen off it again onto his back. He didn't seem to have the strength to try again. He lay with his eyes closed, panting and whimpering.

Afra bent down beside him. She could see the puppy clearly now that it was properly light. He was pathetically thin, no more than a little framework of bones covered with scrappy golden-brown fur, and there was an ugly gash on his left foreleg.

'Whoa there,' said Afra, making her voice as gentle and reassuring as she could. 'What happened to you? It looks like they deserted you. But you're too little to manage on your own. Come on, don't worry. I'm not going to leave you here like this.'

She put out her hand. The puppy seemed too weak now to try and snarl. He cocked one pointed fuzzy ear, but barely lifted his head from the dust. Afra leaned forward and scooped him up into her hands.

'It's breakfast time for you too,' she said.

She became aware of movement behind her and looked up. She had been concentrating so closely on the puppy that she hadn't noticed the crowd of ragged children who had gathered behind her. They stood around her now, staring at her with curious, unsmiling faces. One of them put out a hand to touch her sleeve and began to speak in rapid Amharic.

Afra looked down the lane. Tom was out of sight. He must have reached the inn already. She was on her own.

3

A STARVING PUPPY

Afra stood up, holding the puppy protectively against her chest. She was afraid. The children didn't look hostile, exactly, but they didn't look particularly friendly either. One of them pointed to the puppy and frowned.

'I found him,' said Afra. 'Look, he's starving.'

They didn't seem to understand. One of them said something in Amharic, and a few of the others burst out laughing. Two boys put out their hands to touch the puppy, but Afra snatched him back out of reach.

'Don't!' she said. 'You'll hurt him. Who does he belong to?'

The boys tried to touch the puppy again. Afra felt her temper welling up.

'Back off, will you? Can't you see he's starving? You'll terrify him! He's lost and he needs help, not a whole lot of noisy people pawing at him.'

The anger in her voice had a bad effect on the others. They began to look angry too. The boys who had tried to touch the puppy began to talk excitedly in Amharic.

Afra hadn't noticed a tall quiet boy in a red

sweatshirt and blue baseball cap who had been standing at the back of the crowd, but now he pushed his way to the front.

'Hello,' he said in clear but heavily accented English. 'What is your name? Which country do you come from?'

Afra looked up at him gratefully.

'I'm Afra,' she said. 'I'm from Kenya. My dad's American.' She paused and took a breath. 'My mother is – was – Ethiopian.'

The boy's eyes opened in surprise.

'So you're Ethiopian too,' he said. 'Welcome to my country. It is your country too, of course. Oh, and I am Kassa.'

Afra felt a rush of pleasure and her face broke open into a beaming smile. The boy smiled back at her. She could feel the tension in the crowd of children ebb away. They had obviously understood a little of what she had said. She could hear some of them repeat 'Kenya' and 'American' to each other.

Kassa was looking down at the puppy.

'Is he your dog?' he said, puzzled.

'No.' Afra looked down at the puppy too. He was worryingly thin and passive in her arms and his breathing was laboured. 'I found him. Look, he's hurt. And he's half starved.' She opened her hands to show Kassa the gash on the puppy's foreleg and his skeletal little frame. Kassa sucked his breath in through his teeth sympathetically.

'Do you know who he belongs to?' Afra asked him.

Kassa shook his head. He turned to the other children and fired off some questions in Amharic. They crowded in again to look at the puppy, but Afra didn't mind now. She could see that they weren't distressing him and that their sympathy was engaged.

A girl at the edge of the crowd spoke up and Kassa translated.

'She said, this puppy, he has no home. There was a man there in that house before.' He pointed to a house nearby where the window was shuttered and the door padlocked. 'He had a dog and it had many puppies. He went away one week ago, and the dog went also. Perhaps the puppy was left behind.'

Afra scowled. Indignation was boiling up inside her and she wanted to launch into a furious speech, but she bit back the words. Being angry wouldn't help the puppy, and that was all that mattered now.

'So he doesn't belong to anyone?' she said.

Kassa translated the question. Heads were shaking now and a babble of chatter broke out.

'They say, give him some milk, give him a piece of meat. You have to wash his leg,' Kassa said.

'What's happening? Are you OK?'

Tom's anxious voice broke in from the back of

the crowd, and the children parted to let him through.

Afra made a rueful face at him.

'Sure, I'm OK. But I just got myself a puppy.'

Tom's mouth fell open.

'Afra, you can't! Prof'll do his nut!'

Afra's brows twitched together.

'He'll just have to do it then. Look at him, Tom. He's in real, real trouble here. We can't leave him to starve to death all on his own.'

Tom touched the puppy's head with a gentle forefinger. The puppy opened one bleary eye and gave a faint yelp.

'No,' he said positively. 'Of course we can't. Maybe we can keep him for a bit, anyway, till you find his owner.'

'His owner left town, the cruel monster. He just abandoned him.' An ominous red flush was rising in Afra's cheeks.

'All right, all right,' said Tom hastily. He knew what Afra was like when her fury was aroused. 'Look, if you're going to adopt him, you'd better do something right now. He's looking kind of wobbly to me.'

Afra had already started walking towards the inn. The children began to follow, streaming down the lane like the tail of a comet, and more were running up to see what was happening. Kassa suddenly took control. He turned and said something sharp, and the children stopped. Some gave a final wave and walked away. The others went on following at a distance.

'Thanks,' said Tom, looking appraisingly at Kassa. Kassa was weighing him up too.

'What's your name?' they both said at the same time, and laughed.

'I am Kassa,' said Kassa.

'I'm Tom,' said Tom.

Afra had hurried on and had reached the door of the inn. Beyond the lower courtyard a door led into the bar. She pushed through the plastic fronds that hung across the doorway and looked round for the landlord.

A table was set near the window and some bread was already out on a plate. The landlord came out from a door at the back of the bar. He was carrying two plates, each of which contained five sizzling fried eggs. He saw Tom and began chuckling at once.

'*Dabo*,' he said, pointing at the table. 'He held up the plate for Tom to see, then put it down on the table. '*Inkolal*.'

Tom looked triumphantly at Afra.

'Breakfast,' he said. 'I ordered it.' He took in the plateful of eggs. 'Wow. I didn't think we'd get so many though.'

Afra didn't answer. She was looking anxiously down at the puppy, but Kassa, who had followed them into the bar, looked impressed.

'You can speak Amharic, Tom?'

Tom waggled his head and made a funny face.

'Oh sure. *Dabo*, *inkolal* and I've forgotten the other one.'

The landlord came up to the table with two small glasses of tea.

'*Shai*,' he said.

'That's it, *shai*,' said Tom. 'That's all I can say.'

'I wish you could say milk,' said Afra. 'Kassa, can you ask him to bring some in a bowl? And some clean water?'

The landlord had caught sight of the puppy in Afra's lap, and his smile faded. He said something quietly to Kassa. Kassa looked uncomfortable.

'He says that dogs are not permitted in the bar,' he said. 'It's for reasons of being clean.'

Afra looked longingly at the dish of eggs in front of her, but stood up resolutely.

'OK. I'll take him upstairs to the top courtyard.'

The landlord had bent forward to look more closely at the puppy. He clicked his tongue sympathetically and pressed Afra's shoulder down so that she sank back onto her seat. He spoke to Kassa again.

Kassa grinned.

'He says this is not a dog, it is a sick little thing. We will bring him first some water and then some milk. I do not know about puppies. Perhaps he needs food first.'

Afra shook her head.

'No, he's right. Water, then a little milk. You have to go slowly at first or we could upset his stomach.'

'She knows about animals,' said Tom with a tinge of pride in his voice. 'You should see the animals she's got at home. There's a bushbaby, and a goose, and a swift – only he's old enough to fly around on his own now. And a goat, only he belongs to our friend Joseph really.' He sat down at the table and started attacking the plateful of eggs.

'Hey, this is good. I'm so hungry.'

He felt Afra's reproachful eyes on him and put down his knife and fork.

'Oh sorry,' he said. 'Would you like some, Kassa?'

Kassa raised his hands.

'No, I have eaten my breakfast.'

The landlord came in with a bowl of water and a glass of milk. Afra picked up the spoon and tried to pour a little water into the puppy's mouth. It trickled out. She tried again. This time, the puppy's small pink tongue appeared and he feebly licked a few drops off his nose. Afra dripped in another spoonful. The puppy raised his head and the little circle of watchers saw him swallow.

'He's getting the idea,' breathed Afra. 'Well done, little guy.'

The puppy was whining again, looking up pleadingly at Afra. She poured another spoonful into his mouth. He swallowed more strongly this time.

'You can do it yourself,' she said.

She put the bowl of water on the floor and gently set the puppy down beside it. He staggered to his feet and, lowering his face into the bowl, began to lap.

The anxious watchers crowed with delight.

'He'll do OK now,' said Afra with satisfaction.

She poured a little of the milk into the water. The puppy was drinking enthusiastically now, splashing his forepaws with milk and water.

Afra dragged her eyes away from him.

'Oh wow, am I hungry! Pass the salt, Tom.'

A few minutes later, Tom's plate was empty, and Afra was pushing the last piece of bread round hers to mop up the remains of the egg yolks. The puppy had flopped down onto his stomach beside the empty bowl and was feebly licking his wounded leg.

Afra picked him up and looked at the cut closely.

'Licking's the best thing for it,' she said. 'It's deep but it's not infected. Probably best to leave it to nature. He'd only tear off a bandage, and it wouldn't do any good anyway.'

Kassa was impressed.

'Tom is right. You know about animals,' he said.

There was a rattling noise by the door as

someone pushed through the plastic fronds and came into the bar. Afra and Tom looked round anxiously, then relaxed again as they saw a couple of strangers.

'I thought it was Prof,' said Afra. 'Listen, Tom, we have to hide him, at least while we feed him up a bit and he gets stronger. Come on upstairs with us, Kassa.'

'Why do we have to hide him? Prof wouldn't just kick him out and let him die, would he?' said Tom, shocked.

Afra was already halfway out of the bar.

'No, but he'll get all fussy about us catching fleas and diseases off him and stuff, and try to make us give him to someone else to look after who mightn't do it properly.' She thought of something, and turned to Kassa. 'How do you say "dog" in Amharic, Kassa?'

'*Wusha*,' said Kassa.

Afra nodded.

'That's a cool name. OK, little guy. Your new name is Wusha.'

4
THE WILD WOLVES OF ETHIOPIA

Kassa looked round approvingly at the little courtyard at the top of the stairs. It was shaded by two small trees, and some white plastic tables and chairs were set out under them.

'This is my first time to come in here,' he said, 'even I have lived all my life in Lalibela. Tourist people, they go all the time to the big hotels – very nice en suite there, and *faranji* food.'

Afra and Tom exchanged puzzled looks.

'What food?' said Afra.

'*Faranji*. It means foreigner. It is how we say foreigner in Amharic.'

'How come you speak such brilliant English, Kassa?' asked Tom. 'The other kids down there in the street didn't seem to understand anything.'

'I know many *faranji*s.' Kassa put back his thin shoulders with pride. 'My father takes tourists up into the mountains, to the old monasteries and churches near Lalibela, and when it is not school time I go with him, to help him with the mules. The *faranji*s, they speak to me in English, and I learn like that.'

Afra had settled herself on one of the plastic

chairs with Wusha in her lap. The puppy had fallen asleep, one paw lying in complete relaxation across Afra's hand. She looked up at Kassa.

'You have mules?' she said, respect in her voice.

'Yes,' Kassa said. 'There is one, the best one, it is called Mamete. She is a very nice mule. She is always the one I lead. When I call to her, she will follow me. Her colour is white and she has—'

Tom had been bending over to watch a column of ants that were marching in a straight line across the courtyard, but he suddenly stood upright as if he'd only just heard what Kassa had been saying.

'You go up into the mountains?' he said to Kassa. 'Into the really wild bits?'

'Wild, yes.' Kassa nodded. 'It is wild in the mountains, and cold also.'

'You haven't seen any wolves up there, have you?' Tom said eagerly.

Kassa laughed.

'Wolf? You mean like a big dog? There is no wolf in Ethiopia. Only hyena and jackal and Simien fox.'

'Simien fox!' Tom pounced on the words. 'But they're the ones I mean. They're really wolves! I mean they've always been called foxes, because they're red, but they're not foxes at all. They're wolves.'

Kassa had been trying to follow this.

'You mean a wolf is a fox?'

'No, it's just that they're called that in Ethiopia,' said Tom. 'It's a bit confusing, I know.'

Kassa looked more puzzled than ever.

Wusha gave a snuffling sigh then jerked awake all of a sudden. He opened his eyes wide and looked round as if something had startled him, then he became aware of Afra's hand lying across his tummy and, turning his head round, he tried to gnaw at it with his sharp little teeth.

Afra gently removed her hand.

'He is a good dog,' said Kassa approvingly. 'He will be fierce and bite thieves. Ethiopian dogs, they are all fierce.'

'He'll have to be properly trained,' said Afra firmly, 'and I guess learning who's a thief and who isn't is going to have to be lesson one. Anyway, right now it's time to feed him something a little more exciting than milk and water. Let's go see if the landlord has any real food for him.'

'No, hang on a minute!' Tom had been waiting impatiently to get Kassa's attention again. 'You haven't seen a wolf – I mean, a Simien fox – yourself, have you?'

Kassa patted his chest proudly.

'I have! They are very rare – so rare, only four or five hundred are left in the whole world – and they exist only in Ethiopia. Until just one or two years ago, everyone thought they had all gone from around Lalibela. Then an expert came, Mr Claudio. He asked my father, "Take me to look

34

for Simien fox." I go too, and we find one, then two, then so many – up to fifteen or twenty! The farmers, they know where they are. They tell us where we can go to find them.'

'You've seen them? The wild wolves of Ethiopia?' Tom was awestruck. 'Afra, listen. Why don't we—'

'I know what you're going to say,' Afra interrupted. 'You want us to get Prof to say we can go up there and look for them too.'

She seemed reluctant. Tom was astonished. He had never known Afra sound doubtful about looking for a rare and special animal before.

'What's up with you?' he said. 'You mean you don't want to see them?'

She was looking down again at Wusha, who had stopped trying to bite her and was busily licking her thumb.

'No, no, of course I do,' she said. She felt confused herself. If she'd been anywhere else in the whole world she'd have given anything for a chance to see wolves in the wild, but here, now, she was afraid of being diverted from her real purpose. For once, her quarry was human.

'Well, I'm going to ask Prof anyway,' said Tom, raising his eyebrows and shaking his head in a gesture of bemusement.

A whine from Wusha gave Afra the chance to change the subject.

'Really, I have to get him something to eat now,'

she said. 'A little meat, maybe, cut up fine, and some bread soaked in milk.'

She went off down the stairs, relieved to get away from the others.

She was nearly at the bottom when the door from the street opened and Prof and Giorgis came into the lower courtyard.

Afra froze. Why were they back so early? Surely they hadn't been away for a whole hour and a half!

'You're back!' she said, trying to keep the dismay from showing in her voice.

Prof looked up at her quizzically.

'Well now, and I thought you'd be pleased.' His eyes fell on Wusha, who was wriggling weakly in Afra's hands. 'Ah, I see. A new protégé.' He came up a couple of steps and examined the puppy more closely. 'Why, the poor little creature. He's nothing but skin and bone. He looks half starved.'

She looked up at him hopefully.

'He is, Prof. He desperately needs—'

Prof put his hands up as if he was fending something off.

'Oh no, no, Afra. Not a puppy. Not right now. If you absolutely insist, when we get back to Nairobi I can find one for you, but here . . .'

Afra looked over his shoulder. The landlord had emerged from the bar with a bowl in his hands. He beckoned to Afra.

'I'm just going to make sure he gets something to eat,' she said, pushing past Prof.

'Oh, I see.' Prof sounded relieved. 'He belongs to Worku here. He looked at the landlord who said something to him in Amharic. Prof turned back to Afra. There was a resigned look on his face.

'He seems to think you promised to feed this puppy and told him I'd pay whatever it costs. I presume, on past experience, that that's exactly what you did do?'

'Yes, as a matter of fact, it is,' said Afra defiantly. 'Just look at him, Prof! How could anyone, *anyone*, be hard-hearted enough not to help him? A little guy like this?'

Prof laughed, and Afra could see that behind him Giorgis was smiling too.

'OK, honey. You win. Feed the little fellow as much as you like and get him up on his feet again. As long as we don't have him with us in our baggage when we go home to Nairobi.'

Afra slipped past him without meeting his eyes. She knew how to manage Prof when it came to adopting animals. You had to go slowly, fight one little battle at a time, let him get used to the idea, and give things a chance to just sort of establish themselves.

'Don't worry, Wusha, it's going to be all right,' she whispered as she peered into the bowl in Worku's hands.

'Looks like only bread and milk,' she said, frowning. 'He needs a little meat too.'

Worku looked blankly at her. Prof had gone on up the stairs, but Giorgis, his face full of amusement, had followed her over to the landlord. He said something to him in Amharic.

'*Ishi, ishi*, yes,' Worku said, ducking his head and grinning, obviously surprised at the interest one little puppy was arousing in his guests.

'He'll bring it up in a minute,' said Giorgis, taking the bowl out of Worku's hands. 'Come upstairs again. Your father and I have something to tell you.'

At once Afra forgot the warm little bundle in her hands. An invisible spoon seemed to be stirring her insides.

'About . . . my uncle?' she said.

'Maybe. Just possibly, yes,' Giorgis said, urging her with a nod of the head to go up the stairs in front of him.

Afra almost stumbled in her eagerness to reach the top and find out more, and she had to make herself go slowly in case she fell and hurt Wusha.

'The likeness in the eyes – really it is extraordinary,' she heard Giorgis murmur as he came up behind her, and a warm glow settled round her heart.

Prof had opened the padlock that fastened the battered wooden door to their room and gone inside. He came out a moment later without his thick jacket and warm scarf. Afra realized suddenly that she was hot too. Now that the sun was high in the sky, the air had warmed to a perfect balminess. She set Wusha down on the ground and took her thick sweater off, then looked expectantly at the two men, who had sat down at one of the tables.

Neither of them spoke for a moment.

'What?' she said, unable to bear the suspense any longer. 'What is it?'

Prof tilted his glasses down on his nose and looked at her anxiously over the metal rims.

'Listen, honey. I can't bear for you to get all excited and then be disappointed.'

He stopped. Afra wanted to shout at him to go on, but she held herself back with an effort.

'It's Seyoum, isn't it?' she said as calmly as she could. 'You've got news of Uncle Seyoum?'

'Not exactly,' said Giorgis. He caught sight of Worku's head at the bottom of the stairs and clapped his hands to attract his attention. 'You want some breakfast, Richard?'

Prof nodded. Giorgis gave some rapid instructions while Afra seethed with impatience.

'It's just that I have a friend, a colleague, who is also working on the historical survey,' he went on at last. 'He's here at the moment, not in Lalibela but at a monastery around ten kilometres from here. He was in Germany. He escaped from Ethiopia and found his way there at the time of the Red Terror.' He paused for an agonizing moment. 'He mentioned Seyoum to me in a letter. He'd met up with him in Germany. Seyoum had escaped later, when the fighting got really bad around here.'

Afra gave a shuddering sigh.

'Then he's alive!' she said. Her voice felt tight.

'Honey, we don't know that,' Prof said. 'He *was* alive, but all of this happened a long time ago. He might easily have come back here and got caught up in the fighting. And if he was alive, why didn't he try to find us? It wouldn't have been so difficult. There aren't that many archaeologists called Richard Tovey in the world.'

Afra was staring at him with painful intensity.

'But he'd have looked in America! He wouldn't know you'd gone to live in Kenya.'

Giorgis and Prof exchanged glances.

'It's possible, yes,' Giorgis said cautiously.

'Anyway, can't we look for this friend? Can't we go to the monastery, or whatever, where he is, and at least *ask* him?'

To her surprise, Prof nodded.

'Guess what? Something told me you'd want to do just that. So I suggest that this afternoon we try and get us some mules and a guide, and first thing tomorrow we set off for the monastery in search of . . . What was his name, Giorgis?'

'Taddesse,' said Giorgis, blinking at the sudden radiance that had transfigured Afra's face.

Neither of them saw that, at the mention of mules and guides, Kassa and Tom had turned to each other with delighted smiles.

5

HIDING WUSHA

'If there's one thing Prof's really good at,' Afra said with pride to Tom as they sat alone in the bar eating big bowlfuls of spaghetti, 'it's organizing an expedition. You have to do it all the time if you're an archaeologist.'

Tom was sucking a very long piece of spaghetti through his pursed lips. It had only been three hours since his breakfast of eggs, but he was quite hungry enough for a big lunch of pasta now.

'Yes, I know. He's brilliant,' he said as soon as he could speak. 'I just hope he'll get Kassa's dad to take us. I want to see Mamete.'

'They've been gone for hours.' Afra looked up at the clock that hung between two brightly-coloured calendars on the wall above the bar. Maybe Kassa's dad's gone out of town.'

She was torn between her longing to go in search of the mysterious Taddesse and her anxiety about leaving Wusha behind. The puppy, who had eaten very little of the food he'd been offered, lay asleep under the table, his chin resting on Afra's shoe.

The plastic fronds rattled and Kassa burst through them.

'It is all arranged!' he said, beaming from ear to ear. 'My father is taking you, and I am coming too!'

Wusha stirred in his sleep and his chin slipped off Afra's shoe. She looked under the table. He had quickly settled back into sleep again. He looked pathetic; a scrawny, helpless little creature.

'Where are Prof and Giorgis?' she said.

'Mr Prof—' began Kassa.

Tom and Afra burst out laughing.

'He's not Mr Prof,' said Afra. 'Just Prof. It's short for Professor.'

Kassa looked doubtful.

'It is polite to say only Prof?'

'Everyone calls him that,' said Tom.

'OK,' Kassa went on. 'Prof and Ato Giorgis—'

'Who?' said Tom. 'What?'

'*Ato*,' said Kassa firmly. 'It means Mr in Amharic, and it is not polite to say only Giorgis when you are younger than he is.'

'Oh, OK.' Afra stored the information away in her mind. 'I don't usually go so big on that kind of stuff, but if that's how it's done in Ethiopia it's fine by me.'

From the lane outside came the sudden hoarse braying of a mule.

'Mamete!' cried Kassa, dashing out of the bar.

Afra scooped up Wusha, tucked him into the

43

crook of her elbow, and followed the others outside.

Three mules and one chestnut-coloured horse stood in the lane. Kassa was holding the bridle of the front mule, a sturdy white animal with a dusty muzzle.

'Is that Mamete?' Tom said.

He sounded disappointed. Afra could see why. She too had built up a picture in her mind of a stunning creature with a silky coat and legs like a racehorse's. A kind of 'supermule'. Mamete was just a mule.

Afra went up to her and tried to stroke her nose, but Mamete had caught the doggy smell of Wusha, lying in Afra's arms, and trampled backwards nervously.

'She does not like dogs,' Kassa explained. 'She is afraid.'

Tom was looking at the short, stocky man holding the other two mules. His cropped curly hair was grizzled and he wore a white *shamma* round his neck and shoulders.

'My father,' said Kassa, following Tom's eyes.

Mamete was still nervously aware of Wusha. She threw her head back suddenly, and her bridle jingled. Wusha struggled in Afra's arms and yapped noisily.

Prof glanced up from his list.

'Take that puppy back into the hotel where he belongs,' he said irritably.

Afra backed away from Mamete and looked at her father thoughtfully.

'When are we leaving?' she said.

'Tomorrow morning. At dawn,' said Prof. 'Look, I've got a lot to do with Petros here' – he nodded towards Kassa's father – 'to get everything ready. Why don't you two get Kassa to show you round Lalibela? It might be your only chance.'

'That'd be brilliant,' said Tom. He was bored with sitting around at the hotel and wanted to get out and do something.

Afra thought quickly.

'Can you give me the key to our room then, Prof?' she said. 'I'll need my sunhat.'

Prof threw her the keys. She caught them and started to go into the hotel, then stopped as if something had just occurred to her.

'Come with me, Tom,' she called out to him. 'The padlock's stiff. I couldn't do it the last time.'

Tom gave her a puzzled look. He'd seen her open the padlock without any problem at least twice already.

'Stiff? But—' he began. Then he read the fierce message in her eyes. 'Oh, OK. I'm coming.'

As soon as they were inside the lower courtyard Afra turned to him.

'What are we going to do?' she hissed.

'Do? We're going off on a trek,' he said.

She shook her mop of curls in exasperation.

'No, with Wusha! What are we going to do about Wusha?'

'Oh. I see.' Tom wrinkled his freckled nose. 'Leave him with the landlord? Worku, or whatever his name is?'

Afra would have clenched her fists if she hadn't been carrying the puppy.

'We can't do that!' she said indignantly. 'Look at him. He's still on the critical list. He needs constant care and food and looking after. Worku won't do any of that. He'll just throw him a few bits of bread and stuff from time to time. Giorgis had to really lean on him to get him to give Wusha any meat.'

Tom looked at her in disbelief.

'You don't mean you're going to stay here with him and not come to the monastery with us?'

Afra raised her eyes despairingly.

'Tom, would you pass up on the chance to go to Shangri-La? Of course I'm coming! It's what I want more than anything in the world!'

'What are you going to do then? You can't bring him with us.'

She had been uncertain, but now, suddenly, she knew what to do.

'Oh, can't I? Why not?'

'Prof wouldn't let you. That's why not.'

'Prof's not going to know. Not until it's too late, anyway. That's why I wanted to talk to you. You've got to help me.'

46

She flashed him her sudden dazzling smile. Tom looked at her warily.

'Afra—' he began.

'It'll be easy.' She was coaxing him now. 'We'll keep him with us tonight in our room—'

'But Prof'll hear him. He'll send him down to Worku.'

'He won't notice him at all! Wusha's so weak, poor little thing, he sleeps all the time anyway, and if he wakes up I'll have some food ready for him and I'll pretend to have a coughing fit to cover the noise.'

'It won't work,' said Tom. 'You know it won't.'

'Yes, it will. Prof never hears a thing when he's asleep. And in the morning I'll make a little nest for Wusha in the top of my rucksack.'

Tom looked at her suspiciously.

'That's just for starters, I suppose. What else do you want me to do?'

'Nothing! Honestly!' She grinned. 'Well, I can't think of anything yet, anyway.'

He frowned.

'You needn't think I'm going to share the blame with you when Prof finds out and blows his top, because I'm not.'

She snorted.

'Coward. He'll make a fuss, but it won't be for long. It never is. And it's bound to work because I'll make sure Wusha's had plenty to eat before we start and he'll be sleeping it off until it's too late to turn back.'

Something occurred to Tom.

'But what about Mamete? She'll smell him and go all temperamental on us, and I don't want to ride a bucking bronco, thank you very much.'

Afra nodded.

'You're right. I hadn't thought of that. That's why I need you, Tom, to have good ideas.'

He knew she was trying to get round him, but he couldn't help feeling a bit flattered all the same.

'Tell you what,' he went on, inspired in spite of himself, 'you could rub something smelly like insect repellent on him. It stinks. Mamete wouldn't get a whiff of dog through all that stuff.'

'That's brilliant! Wow, that's so—' She stopped and grabbed his arm. 'Shh! They're coming now! Get up the stairs, quick! We've got to settle him in our room before we go out.'

The afternoon passed in a daze of glory for Afra. Wusha had settled down at once on the towel she'd laid out for him, given a mighty yawn and fallen asleep. She'd left a bowl of water nearby and knew he'd be all right.

They ran quickly through the maze of lanes and little shops and houses, until they came to the enclosure in the heart of Lalibela, where the mysterious churches lay. Afra followed Kassa and Tom, who were going round Lalibela at top speed, bounding through the labyrinth of clefts and tunnels that linked one incredible rock-hewn church to the next, racing all the time to see what was round each corner. She went more slowly, filling herself with the beauty and power of the place.

'Lalibela, Lalibela,' she whispered, laying a hand on the pink-coloured rock, which was warmed now by the afternoon sun. The very name of the place sounded like a magic spell.

'Who made all this? Who could have done it?' she kept asking Kassa as they peered into one perfect church after another, all of them sculpted from the living rock.

'The priests say it was the angels,' he said.

She could almost believe it.

Once, as she looked down from a high point into a dizzyingly deep pit below, she saw a boy hurry out of the church in the centre of it and disappear seconds later into a tunnel.

'Did you see that boy?' she said to the others. 'He was the one in the church this morning. He was chanting out of that massive book.'

They hadn't noticed him.

'He is a deacon, maybe,' said Kassa. 'He is learning to be a priest.'

I want to know that boy, thought Afra. I want to know everyone and everything in this place, to feel it in my bones.

For the first time she understood how Prof felt about old places.

They walked back to the inn in the last of the fading light.

'Goodbye,' said Kassa. 'I will see you tomorrow.'

Afra, who had been silent for the last half hour, couldn't reply. She didn't want to say a word in case the enchantment that had fallen on her was broken.

It was Wusha who brought her back to normal. Afra could hear him whining as she opened the door, and he came across the floor to her, his whole behind waggling with pleasure.

Tom came in after her.

'Ugh!' he said as he crossed the room.

'What's the matter?'

'I've trodden in something.'

She looked down.

'It's only pee. You can't expect a puppy to train himself. I'd better clear it up, quick.'

She took out some tissues and mopped up the little puddle.

'Dinner time for you,' she said, scratching Wusha on the top of his head. 'Let's go and find Worku. Tom, how am I going to explain to him that I need dog food for the journey?'

'Sign language,' said Tom.

'Sign language? Are you kidding? You want me to do a mime or something? OK, you'd better come with me. You can be Wusha and I'll be me, and we'll act like we're going off on a journey. You can beg for food, and I'll look in my bag, only I won't have anything to give you. Then—'

'Yeah. That'd be good.' Tom, who liked acting, was starting to look enthusiastic. 'Come on, let's give it a try.'

Worku was busy in the kitchen. He watched their mime with bafflement, shaking his head and laughing.

'It's no good,' said Afra despondently. 'He isn't getting it at all.'

Finally they all gave up trying. Wusha had been sitting quietly by the door but he gave a little bark as someone came into the courtyard. Worku looked up and noticed him. He reached up to a shelf and brought down a bowl full of pieces of bread soaked in milk. He put it down next to Wusha and handed Afra a plastic bag full of food. Afra looked inside it. There were pieces of bread, a small tin of milk powder, and some paper that looked as if it was wrapped round a piece of liver.

'Journey,' he said. 'Tomorrow. Wusha.'

Afra and Tom burst out laughing.

'I didn't know you could speak English,' Afra said.

He looked at her blankly.

'Maybe his English is like my Amharic,' said Tom.

Afra wasn't listening. She was looking down at

Wusha who was enthusiastically demolishing the contents of the bowl.

'Look at that,' she said admiringly. 'He's really found his appetite now. I guess all we have to do is keep filling him up.'

In the end, the night wasn't as bad as Afra had feared. Prof packed her and Tom off to bed early.

'There'll be a long ride tomorrow, and we're starting early,' he said. 'Go get your beauty sleep.'

'What about your beauty sleep?' asked Afra. She was hoping, for once, that Prof would go off for the evening. She needed time to sort out Wusha.

'Giorgis is coming by for a while. Don't worry, honey. I'll only be downstairs in the bar.'

She smiled at him, pretending to look relieved.

The naked bulb hanging from the ceiling in their room gave out only a dim light, but Tom and Afra worked as quickly and efficiently as they could, making a comfortable travelling bed for Wusha in Afra's bag, afraid all the time that Prof might come in unexpectedly.

When everything was ready and Wusha had had his last little meal, Afra made him comfortable on the towel on her bed and climbed in under the blanket. Tom was in bed already.

'Good night,' she said.

He didn't answer. He had fallen asleep at once.

Afra lay looking up into the dark. A light was

on in the courtyard, and strips of brightness penetrated the room round the edges of the poorly fitting door. Images from the day crowded through her mind – churches and people and a ragged little puppy – but on the edges were shadowy figures, waiting to step forward into the light; the mysterious Taddesse, her long-lost Uncle Seyoum and, up on the high mountain tops, the last red wolves of Ethiopia.

The bleeping of Prof's alarm clock dragged Afra out of a deep sleep. She heard a snuffle and a doggy yawn beside her and was instantly awake and on her guard. Luckily, Prof was groaning himself, drowning out Wusha's noise.

To Afra's relief, Prof, still clumsy with sleepiness, was too worried about getting off to an early start to notice much else. He dressed quickly and went outside to see if Petros and Kassa had arrived with the mules.

'Quick, Tom! Where's Wusha's food?' said Afra, lifting the puppy down onto the floor. 'He's got to eat before we start.'

'I thought you were supposed to feed dogs only once a day,' grumbled Tom, who was too sleepy himself to be bossed around by Afra.

'Not when they're little,' she said crossly. 'They're like babies. They need to eat little bits all the time.'

'Jimmy's like that,' said Tom, thinking of his

new baby brother with a sudden and unexpected pang of homesickness.

'Tom! Afra!' came Prof's voice from downstairs. 'Come on down here and get some breakfast. We're setting off in ten minutes!'

6

UP ON THE HIGH PLATEAU

The air was sharp with cold as they trotted out of Lalibela, and puffs of steam billowed out of the nostrils of the three mules and the packhorse which, loaded with their bags and equipment, was leading the way.

Tom was riding Mamete. He had hardly ever ridden before and Afra could see he was nervous. He was clearly glad that Kassa was walking close beside him. She was next in the line, on a little brown mule. He seemed more placid than Mamete and less inclined to take offence at the smell of Wusha, which might still be coming hrough the strong whiff of insect repellent she'd rubbed on him.

She rode cautiously, the rucksack with Wusha in it on her back. She was being careful not to jolt him, to move at a steady rhythm which, she hoped, would keep Wusha lulled in sleep. She was conscious all the time of Prof, who was riding behind her, and Petros, bringing up the rear on foot.

The path was narrow, rising steeply out of the little town, and they had to go in single file.

Afra looked round in wonder. She'd assumed, without thinking about it much, that Ethiopia would be like Kenya, but everything was different, strange and wonderful. The view of craggy canyons and distant ranges was so immense that she almost felt dizzy when she looked at it. It had the odd effect of making her feel as small as an ant, and uncomfortably unimportant. The trees were different, too. They were tall, slender eucalyptuses, with grey-green leaves that sparkled when the wind rattled them, giving off a spicy, medicinal smell. The houses, clustered together in little hamlets, were the strangest of all. They were round with mud walls, topped with cones of dark thatch. Smoke was curling up through most of them, making them look like steaming puddings.

They've lit fires inside to make breakfast, I guess, she thought.

Children ran out as they passed, calling 'Faranji! Faranji!' in high-pitched voices, and several times dogs made her sweat with anxiety. They burst out, barking, from behind their thorn fences, and one or two, obviously smelling Wusha, ran alongside her for a while, yelping and jumping up.

'Are you OK, honey?' Prof called out. 'It's so amazing how animals pick you out of a crowd.'

She turned cautiously to give him a half smile, and spurred her mule to trot on faster.

Don't wake up, Wusha, she begged silently. Stay quiet. Stay safe.

Once, Prof called out, 'Look up! Look there!' and they all reined in for a moment to watch a huge eagle as it lazily cruised the high currents of air, the tips of its wings tilted up at the ends.

Kassa called out something to a little boy, no more than four or five years old, who was guarding a flock of six or seven goats not far from the path.

'What did you say to him?' asked Tom.

'I tell him to look after his kids carefully,' said Kassa. 'The eagle can steal them.'

Afra's stomach crisped with fright. If an eagle could snatch a kid, it would make off with a puppy in no time. Up here, in the high mountains, she wouldn't be able to let Wusha out of her sight.

The day wore on and the sun grew hotter. The path wound up and up.

Suddenly, Petros called out a command from the back of the little procession, and Kassa jumped forward and pulled on the horse's bridle to stop him. Afra looked up. They had halted at the foot of what seemed to be a solid wall of rock.

'Lost your way, Petros?' said Prof, swinging his long legs over his mule's back as he dismounted.

Petros, a man of few words, grunted and, pushing past the others, took the horse's bridle out of Kassa's hands.

'Get down,' he said to Tom and Afra. 'Follow after me.'

He scrambled up to a small ledge of rock which Afra hadn't noticed. Incredibly, the fully laden packhorse, with no more fuss than a shake of his mane and a toss of his chestnut head, jumped up after him.

'You can't get a horse up there! It's impossible!' said Afra.

Petros was already up on the next tiny ledge and the horse was scrambling up after him. Tom, staring up at the cliff from below, was looking a little green.

'You OK, Tom?' said Prof, who had given his own mule a push on the rear to start it off up the cliff and was about to climb after it.

Tom tried to smile.

'Yeah, I'm fine. I'm just not too crazy about heights.'

Afra was incredulous.

'You never said that before. Come on, Tom. I mean, if horses and mules can do it—'

Prof silenced her with a look.

'There's no problem, Tom,' he said. 'It happens to the best of men. Now I'm going to go up behind you and guide you, and I'll be there if you take a tumble. OK?'

His deep calm voice seemed to give Tom confidence. He set his teeth and turned to the rock face. Afra looked up and saw Petros peering down anxiously from halfway up the cliff. She felt a sudden chill of fright herself. She was sorry now she'd spoken so sharply to Tom. She was beginning to understand how he felt. The packhorse and Prof's mule seemed to be clinging to the face of the cliff like monkeys, and the top was horribly far away.

'Do they ever fall off?' she asked Kassa, keeping her voice down in case Tom heard.

He nodded seriously, his eyes on the animals above.

'Sometimes, but our mules are very good. Very strong. Often they have been here before.'

Prof and Tom were already well up the cliff. Kassa suddenly leaped into action. He gave Mamete a light smack on the rump with the palm of his hand, and with gutteral shouts of '*Hidj! Hidj!*' sent her up the first jump then drove the other mule after her.

Afra heard a whimper from inside the rucksack on her back. She looked up. Prof and the others were too busy getting up the cliff to notice her. Quickly, she slipped the rucksack off and opened it. Wusha blinked up at her, dazzled by the sudden light, and whined. When she had lifted him out, he lowered his behind and a stream of pee ran out over the ground. She opened one of the pouches at the side of the rucksack and, pulling out a soggy plastic bag, dropped a few pieces of milky bread into the puppy's mouth. He gulped them down greedily.

'Afra! Are you OK? What are you doing? Do you want me to come down and help you?'

She looked up. Incredibly, Prof and Tom had already reached the top. They were leaning over the cliff edge and looking down at her.

Quickly, she put Wusha back in the rucksack. She could hear him snuffling contentedly, settling back on his towel. She hoisted the rucksack onto her back and, her knees feeling suddenly weak, she began to climb.

It wasn't nearly as bad as it had looked from the bottom. It was more like a flight of very steep steps than a real rock climb but, even so, she could hardly believe that horses and mules had made it up here.

She emerged at the top, panting, and Prof hooked his hand under her arm to pull her up the last steep jump. She had to stop herself pushing him away. She was beginning to feel bad about him; to dread not only his anger when he found out about Wusha, but, worse than that, the contempt he would feel for the way she had deceived him.

She suppressed the thought and looked round.

They had entered a different world. A huge open plateau, too high for trees, swept away in front of them, and Afra knew, without having to go and see, that the ground fell away on all sides in cliffs as steep as the one they'd climbed. It was like standing on a table.

Far away, to their left, clouds were billowing up from below, like steam puffing out over the edge of a cauldron.

We're above the clouds! We're in the sky! Afra thought. This is the roof of Africa.

She shivered. She'd been hot climbing the cliff but she was cooling down rapidly now in the cold high air.

'Is it OK if I walk for a bit?' she asked Kassa.

'It is good. It is OK,' he said.

Tom looked relieved.

'I'd like to walk too,' he said. 'I'm going to be as stiff as a board if I go on riding. Don't you want a go on Mamete, Kassa?'

Kassa looked back enquiringly at his father, but Petros frowned and shook his head.

'It is better for me to walk,' Kassa said regretfully, patting Mamete's neck with a loving hand. 'If I am riding I cannot watch out and guide the other mules so easily.'

Afra was enjoying the springiness of the ground underfoot. Grass grew only in sparse clumps, between which sprouted a great variety of small, strange plants with velvety grey leaves or tiny flowers – purple, yellow and white. Dead stems of old shrubs, pale with age, lay between boulders as high as cows, which were mottled with beautiful lichens, some a soft green colour like old moss, others yellow-grey and stiff as corals, and still others which were rosettes of burning orange, spattering the soft grey surface of the rock like splashes of paint.

The sky seems nearer, somehow, thought Afra, looking up into the deep, translucent blue.

From somewhere far away came the faint twittering of birds, but apart from that and the plop of the mules' hoofs on the soft earth, there was silence.

It must always have been like this, she thought. Since the beginning of time.

She could see now that the plateau wasn't as flat as she had thought at first. It undulated gently, rising to shallow hillocks and falling again into dips where water had collected in still ponds. On a low ridge nearby, strange cactus-like plants, higher than a man, whose long stems burst out into fans of spiked leaves, stood out from the low grey vegetation as stiff and straight as soldiers standing to attention.

The wind was bitingly cold.

'This is strong country,' she heard Prof say behind her. 'Living things have to be tough for this.'

At that moment, she saw the wolf.

He was sitting on his haunches no more than thirty metres away, gravely watching them. She stopped dead in her tracks and Tom, who was right behind her, nearly cannoned into her.

'Watch where you're—' he began, then he saw the wolf too, and the breath came out of him in a long, rapturous 'Ohh!'

The horse and mules, with Kassa and Petros, were plodding on, but Afra, Tom and Prof stood side by side, spellbound, watching the wolf as he watched them.

He was a vivid russet colour, more orange than red, his coat luxuriously thick. Above his long fine muzzle his deep amber eyes seemed aloof but not hostile, curious but not friendly. He was not afraid of them.

Casually, as if he had recalled some business elsewhere, the wolf stood up and, turning his head away from them, opened his mouth in a wide yawn. Afra could see his tongue curling backwards like a drake's tail inside his mouth.

He's the master here, she thought.

It hadn't occurred to her to be afraid until the wolf began to trot away, his gait curiously stiff, tilting backwards and forwards as if on a see-saw. But suddenly, in her mind's eye, she saw a pack of hyenas on the trail of a hunted creature, running strongly, relentlessly in pursuit, and she shivered.

'They don't go for people, do they? Like leopards or anything?' Tom asked Kassa, who had come back to join them.

Afra, grateful to him for asking the question, craned forward to hear Kassa's answer.

'No, no,' he said, surprised. 'The Simien fox,

he is very peaceful, very quiet for people. He eats only small, little animals. He digs them up from the ground. Like rats and such things. Even he will not eat lambs or kids, except if he is very hungry. And the farmers, they do not hate him. They like him, really, because he chases the jackals – and the jackals, they will steal the sheep and goats.'

The wolf had disappeared behind the ridge. Afra watched him go with a pang of regret.

'They're kind of lonely, then,' she said.

'No.' Kassa shook his head. 'They have families. They are called . . . There is a word for it but I cannot remember.'

'Packs,' said Tom. 'A pack of wolves.'

'Yes, a pack. Mr Claudio told me this word. They live together with ten or twelve sometimes, and when the chief female has cubs, all the other females look after them – like a nurse or something.'

'Wow!' said Afra. 'That's so cool. Nicer than humans.'

'But the females don't drive the young males away, out of the family, do they?' asked Tom, frowning. 'I knew an elephant once, and all the females in his family chased him away.'

'No.' Kassa squared his shoulders and grinned at Tom. 'Females, they cannot tell a wolf or a man what to do. We are too strong for them. They have to obey us.'

They both looked at Afra with pleasurable anticipation. She didn't rise to the bait. She was anxiously listening to her rucksack where, for the last few minutes, Wusha had been growing restless. His low whines were changing now to piercing, yapping barks.

Afra looked round at Prof. He had heard the barks too, and a thunderous frown was gathering on his face.

7

PROF LOSES HIS TEMPER

Afra watched with her heart in her mouth while comprehension dawned in Prof's eyes.

'Take that rucksack off,' he said. 'Open it, please.'

She tried to look defiant but she was quaking inside. Prof didn't get angry very often, but when he did she always wanted to curl up and die.

She took the rucksack off and opened it. Wusha stopped barking and tried to lick her thumb. She looked down into his creased little face and took courage from it.

'Afra, I don't believe this. You lied to me! You deliberately deceived me!' He was as hard and contemptuous as if she'd been one of his students caught stealing an ancient artefact. 'And after I've set up this whole expedition just for your benefit!'

She was painfully aware of Tom and Kassa, who were looking down at the ground in embarrassment, and of Petros, who had tactfully turned away to tighten the girth on the packhorse. She was humiliated. She didn't know what to say. Trembling, she bent down, picked Wusha up and held him against her chest. It seemed to make Prof angrier than ever.

'I don't know what to do with you!' he burst out, and she was a little relieved to hear the heat in his voice. Explosive anger was easier to deal with than cold disgust. 'As soon as an animal comes into your sights, you lose all sense of proportion – any sense at all, in fact. How could you have had the sheer arrogance to remove what is clearly a small and dependent puppy from its legitimate owner, and no doubt from its own mother, which it still needs? It's theft, on top of everything else, and stupidly irresponsible.'

She saw her chance and found her voice. It came out tight with unshed tears.

'How can you *say* that? How can you even think it? You know I wouldn't do that! I'd *never* take a puppy away from his mother, and if you don't know that you don't know a thing about me!'

They stood and glared at each other.

Tom, who had been feeling awful, cleared his throat and stepped forward bravely.

'It's true, Prof. She asked everyone, all the kids around, and they said the owner had gone off with Wusha's mum and had just left him to die.'

'And he *was* nearly dead!' Afra's indignation was boiling up now. 'We saved him! He's still half starved – which you'd know if you'd bothered to look at him. He needs all the help he can get if he's going to make it, but you couldn't give a damn, could you? You're so mean and hard, you'd have left him in the gutter to die all by himself, without anyone to even stroke him or . . . or comfort him or anything!'

'Afra, you're being dramatic,' said Prof, his lips tightening.

She was infuriated.

'You're just cold and selfish and cruel,' she shouted, 'and you don't care about anyone else in the whole world! If you can't be bothered to save a dying puppy, what kind of a person are you?'

She saw with unhappy satisfaction that she'd hurt him.

'I knew it was a mistake,' he said, his voice arctic again, 'to leave Lalibela on this wild-goose chase. I thought at least that if I went along with it I'd have your cooperation. I was obviously wrong.'

She felt as if he'd slapped her.

'A wild-goose chase? *A wild-goose chase?* You mean you think you're just indulging some little fantasy of mine as if I was a whining baby? You don't believe Taddesse knows anything, do you, and you don't think we're going to find out about Uncle Seyoum at all!'

'No, frankly, I don't,' Prof said. 'I've told you over and over again. Your mother's family's lost. They're gone. You have to accept it.'

For a moment there was a stony silence, then Afra, planting Wusha in Tom's arms, hoisted her rucksack onto her back and retrieved the puppy again.

'Go back then,' she said, and this time the ice was in her voice. 'Go back and spend your time talking about archaeology with Giorgis. That's what you really want, isn't it? That's why you came to Lalibela in the first place. It was nothing to do with me. It's *my* family and I'm going on. I'm going to find Taddesse, and Uncle Seyoum, whatever it takes.'

She turned her back on him and set off down the path again. Tom, looking doubtfully for a moment at Prof's set face, followed her uneasily.

'Oh, Afra, don't be so absurd!' Prof's voice floated after her. 'Of course we're all going on to the monastery!'

'Yes,' she flashed back at him, 'so you can go look at another heap of old stones. That's what you're really coming for, isn't it?'

He didn't answer, but she heard behind her the soft thudding of hoofs as the little cavalcade began to move forward again.

Wusha, restless after so many hours in captivity, was wriggling about, trying to claw his way up her chest to her shoulder. Hot tears were running off Afra's cheeks and dripping onto his golden coat.

I'm on my own, she was thinking. I'll have to

do all this alone. He doesn't even want to *try*. He's not interested in anyone except himself. I thought he was, but now I know he isn't.

'Are you all right?' said Tom, coming up alongside her. He was half hoping she'd thank him for standing up to Prof, but she was too wrapped up in her own thoughts to do more than give him a little nod. A desperate resolve was forming in her mind.

I'll go it alone, she thought. If he won't help me, I'll just take off and follow the trail myself, wherever it leads. I'll spend the rest of my life, if I have to, trying to find out about my mother. For as long as it takes.

She wasn't aware any more of anything around her, of the strange grey plants stretching away to the far edges of the plateau, of the soft snorting breath and jingling bridles of the horse and the mules behind her, or of Tom, who had now fallen behind her and whose boots were crunching on the small loose stones of the path. She'd even forgotten Wusha, who had settled comfortably in her arms.

She had entered a vivid angry daydream. She saw herself, thin and ragged, her shoes in holes, walking from one Ethiopian village to the next, year after weary year, questioning by day the people walking along the road to the market place, and stumbling by night across a bare hillside towards the flickering light of a distant, lonely hut.

'I'll find out if it kills me!' she muttered fiercely.

Tom suddenly leaned forward and grabbed her arm. She tried to shake him off, but he held on and she saw that he was pointing. She looked up.

A wolf was standing below her, no more than twenty paces away. He was rigid with concentration, his head bent down as if he was listening.

Afra held her breath, but the wolf seemed unaware of them. It was moving now, in funny, twisting jumps. Afra could see that there must be a huge warren of burrowing rodents here because the ground was bumpy where the earth had fallen in. The wolf began to dig furiously, scrabbling at the earth with his big forepaws. Then something attracted his attention and he looked up.

A smaller wolf, paler, almost sandy in colour, was strolling nonchalantly past. The bigger, redder wolf, losing interest in his hunt, trotted after her. A moment later they had retreated to high rock a little further away. They were sniffing at each other now, licking each other's faces.

'That's so amazing,' said Afra quietly, letting out her breath. 'They don't seem bothered by us at all.'

'The wind's in our favour,' said Prof, coming up quietly behind her. 'They can't have picked up our scent clearly. If we'd been moving towards them they might have been more alarmed. Look, put that puppy back in your rucksack now. It's too cold for him up here. In his condition he needs to be kept warm.'

She shot him a fleeting look, but he was observing the wolves.

'Where are all the others then, if they're supposed to live in packs?' said Tom.

'They have to go separately for hunting,' answered Kassa. 'That is what Claudio told me. At night-time they meet each other and sleep close, all touching so that they can keep warm. At night it is so cold here. There is ice, and even snow sometimes. But in the day they go off, by one, by one, and hunt for little rodents.'

'It's so weird that they're not scared of us at all,' Tom said.

'Why will they be scared?' said Kassa. 'Ethiopian people do not hurt them. We are not fearful of them and they are not fearful of us.'

Wusha, still in Afra's arms, had been flaring his small black nostrils, investigating the smells that the wind was wafting towards them. He seemed suddenly to catch the wolves' scent, lifted his head, and barked furiously.

The bigger wolf visibly responded. He moved his head from side to side, focusing his eyes on the bundle in Afra's arms. Afra, who had been about to put Wusha back in the rucksack, tightened her grip nervously.

'He wouldn't go for him, would he?'

Kassa looked puzzled.

'You know. Attack him, or anything?'

He shook his head.

'No. Wolves, they are friendly sometimes with dogs. They can play with them, even.'

Petros grunted disapprovingly.

'Wolf and dog together, it is not good.' It was the longest sentence any of them had heard him utter. 'Dogs have many diseases. They give them to the wolf and the wolf dies. Wolf is our Ethiopian wildlife treasure. Only in our country they live.' He looked at Wusha and frowned. 'Keep that dog away from wolf,' he said to Afra with a jerk of the head.

Afra hurriedly returned Wusha to the rucksack. She felt chastened. She'd been afraid only for Wusha. It had never occurred to her that he could bring harm to anyone else.

The wolves seemed to have lost interest in them. By the time Afra had settled Wusha down again and stood up, they were some way away, strutting on their slender elegant legs across the windswept plateau.

'Do you reckon they're mates,' Tom asked Kassa, 'or do you think they belong to the same family? Pack, I mean.'

Kassa shrugged.

'I don't know.'

'You can say family,' said Afra pointedly. 'It's not a dirty word or anything. Packs are families.

73

Wolves need families. All mammals do.' She paused and glowered at Prof. 'Even puppies need families.'

Prof's lips twitched. He looked down at her.

'It's all right, Afra. No need to ram it in. I get the point. What you're trying to say is that girls need families. Am I right?'

'Yes. You are. *Especially* girls.' She realized she might be sounding selfish, and qualified it. 'Well, maybe not especially girls. I mean, no more than other people, but girls definitely do, anyway. And so do little puppies.'

Prof, who seemed at a loss for words, turned to Petros.

'You have any daughters, Petros?'

Petros's cheeks wrinkled up as he smiled. He shook his head.

'Two. They are like their mother. When they are happy, everything is good. When they want something . . .' He threw up his hands.

'I know what you mean,' Prof said with feeling. 'Well, are we going to stay here for ever, or are we going on to look for Taddesse, or what?'

Afra looked at him doubtfully, wondering if it was all over or not.

Kassa seemed to have no doubts.

'You want to ride Mamete now?' he said. He didn't smile at her, and Afra, looking at his face, felt small.

He probably thinks I'm just a spoiled foreign brat, she thought.

She turned to Tom.

'Do you mind? You've been riding her up to now.'

Tom shook his head hastily.

'I wouldn't mind a change,' he said. 'Your mule looks kind of . . .' He was about to say 'quiet', but was afraid of sounding weak. He'd found the high-spirited Mamete quite hard to handle. 'But won't she mind about Wusha?'

'I guess not. She's right close to the rucksack now, look, but she doesn't seem bothered any more. She's probably gotten used to him by now.'

She was about to pick up the rucksack but Prof took it out of her hands.

'I'll take this,' he said. 'I'm going to walk. He'll be safer if he's carried by someone on foot.'

He lifted the flap of the rucksack and tickled Wusha under one ear. Afra felt sudden tears sting the insides of her eyelids.

'I'm sorry, Prof,' she mumbled. 'I should have told you about him. I should have got it all straightened out with you before we left Lalibela.'

For an answer, he hoisted her up onto Mamete's back and patted her knee.

'Let's go,' he said. 'There's still a long ride ahead of us.'

8

THE MONASTERY IN THE MOUNTAINS

The cloud which had been bubbling up over the edge of the plateau had been coming closer and closer without anyone noticing. Now it suddenly overtook them so that Afra and Tom, who were riding at the back of the little procession, found themselves muffled in a damp white blanket of fog.

Prof's voice came floating back to them out of the mist ahead.

'Keep close! Don't get lost!'

The path was wide enough for two mules to ride abreast and Afra was glad when Tom came up alongside her.

'I'm glad that's over,' he said. 'You got round him OK.'

Afra didn't look at him.

'I shouldn't have said all that,' she mumbled.

'All what?' said Tom.

'About him being so selfish and not wanting to find my mother's family.'

'So what? Maybe you were right and he doesn't want to anyway,' said Tom, who was bored with the subject and was peering into the mist hoping to catch the red flash of another wolf.

Afra didn't answer. Her eyes were fixed unseeingly on the rough tuft of mane between Mamete's tall white ears.

OK, she was thinking. Maybe he really doesn't want to find them. And maybe he's got a reason.

She frowned, concentrating hard.

He did meet a few of them – years ago, I think. Maybe he quarrelled with them or something, and he doesn't want to tell me. Maybe they didn't like the thought of her marrying a foreigner. Or perhaps it's just too painful and he's afraid it'll make him feel sad all over again.

She was feeling horribly guilty now.

I've been mean, really mean to him, she thought. I just wish I'd never said all those things.

A patch of bright blue sky suddenly appeared overhead, as if an invisible hand had cut a hole in the cloud blanket. The mist lifted as quickly as it had come. She could see Prof clearly now. He turned, hampered by the rucksack on his back, and waved at her.

'You know something,' he called out, 'I'm almost beginning to believe in this expedition of yours. Just look around you. Isn't it magical up here? Doesn't it feel as if anything – anything at all – could happen?'

Afra's spirits lifted. She knew what Prof was like when he got enthusiastic about something.

Maybe she'd got it wrong and he'd start to feel the way she did and join her in the quest after all.

The path had been going downhill for a little while now and Afra realized that they'd come to the far edge of the plateau. She felt a kick of fear in her stomach as the ground seemed to disappear from under her feet, and a dizzying drop, as steep as the one they'd climbed earlier, was right in front of them.

Petros and the packhorse were already disappearing into what looked like a cleft in the ground. Afra heard Tom, who had fallen behind her, nervously clearing his throat. She looked round at him. There was a greenish tinge to his face.

'It'll be OK,' she said uncertainly, but before she could say anything else, Prof had hurried up alongside her.

'Better get off the mules here,' he said, and although his voice sounded casual Afra could see that he was looking carefully at Tom. 'I'll lead them. You'll find it quite easy once you've started.'

To her surprise, Afra found that he was right. Although the way down was steep and rocky, it wasn't nearly as scary as the way up had been. Even Tom, who was coming down slowly behind Prof, managed to grin at her when she turned to look back at him.

They came off the steepest part of the cliff onto a wide platform of land. Petros and Kassa had already disappeared down the next stretch of path, and Afra could hear the hoofs of the pack-horse clinking and sliding on the stones.

The next half hour was a tiring scramble down the narrow tortuous path. The vegetation had changed already. Instead of the grey-green clumpy plants on top of the plateau, there were real bushes here, growing scrubbily out of the bare earth. They looked stunted, as if they had been nibbled, and Afra, looking around for goats, heard a distant bleating and realized that they had come back down into the realms of humankind.

Her exhilaration had left her and she was suddenly very tired.

The monastery took her by surprise. They came round a corner and found themselves face to face with a rough stone wall. A doorway under a little thatched roof was set into it. The thick wooden door was half open, and through it Afra could see a courtyard. At the far end of it the stone facade of the monastery was set into the cliff, cut like the churches of Lalibela out of the solid rock.

Afra's pulse quickened. A faint smell, a mixture of woodsmoke and some kind of incense, wafted out through the doorway towards her on the crystal-clear air. She heard the murmur of voices. She wanted to dash through the door and see at once if Taddesse was there, but she was suddenly scared.

He won't be here. This is just crazy. I got it all wrong, she thought.

Petros was already unloading the packhorse. Kassa was at Mamete's head, murmuring calmly to her. She was backing away from the door nervously, tossing her head and flattening her ears.

There was a sudden snarl, and a big dog, its teeth bared, came racing up the hill towards them. The brown fur on its neck was raised in anger. It lifted its head and began to bark hysterically.

For a moment it seemed as if all three mules and the horse would turn and take to their heels, but Kassa and Petros were too quick for them. They herded them quickly together and Kassa guarded them while Petros lifted his hand as if he was about to throw a stone at the dog.

A voice from inside called out sharply, and the dog slunk away.

The door swung wide open and a monk, swathed in yellow robes and with a yellow turban tied round his head, came out and asked Petros a sharp question.

Behind him, Afra caught a glimpse of three other Ethiopian men. Two of them were dressed in the same kind of white robes that the priests in Lalibela had worn. But the third, who was sitting with them on a mat sharing a dish of food, was wearing ordinary trousers and a green bomber jacket, and his head was bare.

He looked up and saw them.

'Joachim? *Du bist schon wieder da?*' he said, looking surprised. Then he got to his feet and came to the door, blocking the view of the courtyard.

Prof took the rucksack off and balanced it carefully against the wall. He went towards the young man, his hand held out.

'Sorry,' he said. 'I can't speak German.'

The man laughed.

'I was expecting someone else. A colleague from Germany. You are not from the historical survey?'

'No, no.' Prof shook his head. 'We're here for a completely different reason. Are you by any chance Taddesse? If so, you're the person we've come to find.'

'Sure, I'm Taddesse.'

Afra clasped her hands nervously together. The man was looking surprised, and a little anxious.

'You've come all the way out here to find me?'

'It's a long story,' said Prof. 'We'll tell you all about it.'

Taddesse stood aside to let Prof go in through the doorway. A snuffling noise came from inside the rucksack.

'Hey, that's poor old Wusha,' said Tom.

Afra didn't seem to hear him.

Tom opened the rucksack and took the puppy out.

'They all seem to have forgotten you,' he said pointedly. 'You'll have to make do with me.'

He looked back at Kassa, who was already following Petros towards a group of huts and a brushwood corral a little way down the hillside.

'Aren't you coming in, Kassa?' Tom called out.

Kassa shook his head.

'I am looking after Mamete,' he said proudly. 'It is my job.'

Tom turned to Afra. She hadn't followed Prof inside. She was still staring through the doorway of the monastery with a peculiar look on her face as if she was under a spell.

'Wait, Kassa, I'll come and help you,' called Tom, and carrying the puppy he followed the mules towards the corral. Afra, suddenly spurred into motion, darted after Prof. He put his arm round her shoulders and pulled her forwards to stand beside him.

'My name's Richard Tovey,' he said. 'And this is my daughter, Afra.'

Taddesse was looking at him in astonishment.

'Tovey? You are Professor Tovey? I have read your book on archaeology. *An Archaeological Survey of the Middle Ages in East Africa*. It is very fine. And you have come here to find me? Please, sit down.'

He pointed to the mat. Prof sat down. Afra stood beside him, her eyes fixed on Taddesse.

Taddesse turned to the oldest of the robed men and said something rapidly in Amharic. The man had been looking aloof and a little disapproving, but his face broke open into a smile and he leaned forward to shake Prof's hand.

'We've come here on quite a strange mission,' said Prof, pulling Afra down to sit beside him on the mat. 'We're looking for someone. For Seyoum Habtewold.'

'Seyoum Habtewold?' Taddesse sat down too. He was looking more and more bewildered. 'But he is not here.'

'Well no,' said Prof. 'I didn't expect to find him. I just thought – Afra just thought – that you might be able to tell us something about him. Look, I'd better tell you what this is all about.'

Afra suddenly found her voice.

'Seyoum is my uncle,' she said in a rush. 'Only I've never met him. My mom died when I was born. She was Ethiopian and Seyoum was her brother. We came here to find my mother's family. We met this guy in Lalibela, Ato Giorgis – he's an old friend of my dad's – and he said maybe you could tell us something because you and Seyoum used to be good friends.'

Taddesse, who had seemed overwhelmed by meeting Prof, now seemed equally astonished by Afra.

'You are Sablay's daughter?'

'You knew her?' Afra's voice was so tight she could barely speak. The vision she'd been following, which had seemed at times no more than an insubstantial wraith, had fluttered once again across her path of vision.

'Of course I knew her,' Taddesse said. 'But it was many years ago. And Seyoum, I have not seen him since nine, maybe ten years ago. I am sorry. You have come so far to find him. But I cannot help you. I do not know anything at all.'

9

AFRA IS DISAPPOINTED

It took a moment for Afra to understand what Taddesse had said, and when she did the disappointment was so great she couldn't comprehend it. She'd felt a kind of magic drawing her in as she'd looked through the doorway into the monastery courtyard, and she'd been quite certain at that moment that her quest would end here.

'But you must know where he is!' she cried, and the words came out in a despairing wail.

Taddesse looked uncomfortable and spread out his hands apologetically. The priests were watching curiously. One of them turned and tapped Taddesse on the arm as if he was asking for an explanation. Taddesse spoke to him for a moment in Amharic. The priest shook his head and clicked his tongue sympathetically, then he looked at Afra with renewed interest.

'There is a man perhaps in Makelle who can help you,' Taddesse said without conviction. 'He was in Holland, I think, some five or seven years ago. Maybe he will know . . .' His voice tailed off.

Afra swallowed hard. She was making a superhuman effort to control the feelings that were boiling up inside her. She wanted to scream and shout and find someone to blame, or at the very least to burst into a storm of tears. But she had to keep calm. Quests were like this. Barriers came across the way. Dangers and pitfalls had to be faced. Everyone would expect her to behave like a baby now, to have a tantrum and then to give up, to turn back and admit that the search had failed. She wouldn't do it. There had to be a next step, another door to open, and she was going to find it.

She felt Prof's hand on her shoulder and knew by its gentle pressure that his face was full of sympathy. She didn't dare look at him in case he weakened her resolve and made her cry. She had to keep thinking clearly, to make another plan.

'You knew Seyoum well though, didn't you, Ato Taddesse,' she said, trying to keep her voice low and polite and looking earnestly up at Taddesse, who was taken aback by the intensity in her eyes. 'How did you know him? Where did you meet him? What was he doing?'

'Giorgis told us, honey. Don't you remember?' said Prof. 'They met up in Germany.'

Afra suppressed a spurt of irritation.

'Please, Prof,' she whispered. 'Let me do this.'

Taddesse shifted his slim shoulders as he concentrated on her questions.

'You are right. It was in Germany. We were at the university in Berlin.'

'You mean he was studying there? He was a student?' asked Afra, feeling her way.

'Yes. Before, he was at the university in Addis Ababa. That was when things became very bad in Ethiopia. Politically bad. He had to escape from there before he finished his studies. He had to go out of the country.'

'What was he studying?' Afra was casting around like a dog looking for a scent, not knowing what questions to ask.

'Economics, I think,' said Taddesse. 'But it was hard for him in Germany. He was not so good at learning the language. He got an opportunity to go somewhere else. Perhaps it was Holland, or Britain maybe. Or perhaps the US. He left Berlin after one year, and I didn't see him again.'

'Economics,' repeated Afra, seizing on the word as if it might contain hidden treasures to be unearthed. 'What do you do after you've studied economics? I mean, isn't there some special job or something everyone does afterwards?'

'Some of them, they become businessmen,' Taddesse said doubtfully. 'Or perhaps they work for some government agency. There are so many things they can do.'

Afra couldn't keep it up. Her heart was sinking lower and lower. She was beginning to feel as if a heavy weight was pushing down on her head.

I mustn't stop, she told herself desperately. I'll

think of something. There has to be a way out of this.

Suddenly she felt she had to move. She had to take action. She jumped to her feet.

'We're wasting time here! Prof, we have to go back to Lalibela at once! I'll go get Petros and the mules.'

She was about to run back out through the door in the wall.

'Whoa! Wait a minute.' Prof caught hold of her hand and stopped her in mid-flight. 'We can't go anywhere tonight. It's late now. Think of climbing up and down the cliffs in the dark. Anyway, the mules have to rest.'

Afra wanted to say something biting, but she knew he was right. She looked at him helplessly.

'Oh, honey,' said Prof. 'I'm sorry. I wish it hadn't ended up this way.'

'It hasn't ended!' she said fiercely. 'It'll never end – not ever, ever, as long as I live!'

He was shaking his head gently at her, but the expression in his face was so kind and loving she knew she was about to cry. Fortunately, at that moment Tom came back through the doorway into the courtyard. Wusha was in his arms.

'Does he know him? Seyoum, I mean?' he asked Afra.

She couldn't answer. She shook her head.

'Oh, what a pain,' said Tom cheerfully. 'What do we do next? Go back to Lalibela, I suppose, and ask Giorgis if he's got any more ideas. He's so clued up, I bet he'll have millions of suggestions.'

His blithe confidence was infectious. Afra managed a shaky smile.

'Wow, Tom,' she said. 'You're just so great, you know that? You're right. We'll go back to Giorgis. He'll have some more ideas, I know he will.'

Tom smirked, pleased with himself.

'When are we going then? Tomorrow?'

'Yes,' said Afra eagerly. 'Let's start real early and try to catch Giorgis tomorrow evening.'

Kassa and Petros had come in behind Tom. Petros was shaking his head.

'Tomorrow, it is no good,' he said. 'The mules, they are very tired, and the packhorse has a sore place on his back. Tomorrow they must rest, for one day or maybe for two.'

Afra felt a surge of blind unreasoning anger. She closed her eyes for a moment, then opened them again and said, as calmly as she could, 'We can't waste a whole day here. We'll just have to walk back to Lalibela. We could manage without the mules. We could leave them here and—'

'Afra, are you crazy?' interrupted Tom, setting Wusha down on the ground. 'We'd never find the way, unless you've got some amazing magnetic compass in your head you never told me about. I don't know about you, but I don't fancy being lost in the mountains in the middle of Ethiopia, thank you very much.'

'OK, wise guy.' Afra took refuge in sarcasm. 'I may not have some wacky computer chip direction-finder plumbed into my brain, but Kassa has. More or less, anyway. He knows his way blindfold all over these mountains. He could guide us on foot, and Petros could take the mules back when they're rested.'

She looked pleadingly at Kassa, but his eyes were on his father.

Petros raised his chin in a dismissive gesture.

'It is not possible. Two men to go with the mules is necessary.'

'Make your mind up to it, honey,' said Prof. 'We have no choice. We must stay here tomorrow and let the mules rest. Giorgis will still be there when we get back to Lalibela. It'll wait till then.'

His tone was patronizing. It flicked Afra on the raw and her superhuman effort to stay calm and in control deserted her.

'Prof, why are you doing this? You just keep blocking me all the time! As far as you're concerned, I could wait for ever. Well I'm not going to! OK, so we have to stay here one more day, but when we get back to Lalibela I'm just going to keep on trying, and nobody's going to stop me.'

She became aware of the shocked expressions on the faces of Taddesse and the priests, and she stopped and looked down, anxious not to forfeit their good opinion. She thought they might be shocked if an Ethiopian girl spoke to her father like that.

Taddesse broke the silence.

'This young man is your son?' he said to Prof.

'You mean Tom?' said Prof. 'No, he's our friend.'

'My best friend,' murmured Afra, looking gratefully at Tom.

No one had noticed Wusha, and now he began to whine and tussle at Afra's shoe. She bent down and picked him up, holding him close to her chest as if she needed all the comfort he could give her.

'You're hungry,' she said 'You must eat.'

She turned her back on the others, opened her rucksack and pulled out Wusha's bowl. Then she began to mix some milk powder with water from her bottle.

The two priests and the monk were talking together. Prof went to sit with them, joining in their conversation in his halting Amharic. He got up after a few minutes and went across to Afra.

'Listen,' he said. 'We have a problem. They're being very kind. They've told us we can pitch our tent just outside the monastery walls, but Wusha can't stay here inside the courtyard. You have to take him out.'

Afra, who had been feeding Wusha by hand with tiny pieces of meat, looked over her shoulder at him.

'What do you mean? Why?'

'Now listen, Afra.' Prof raised a warning forefinger. 'There's no question about this one. We're in a monastery here. It's holy ground. And in Ethiopia dogs are not permitted in places like this.'

Afra digested this in silence. Then, with a polite little bow towards the priests, and with as much dignity as she could muster, she picked up the puppy and the bowl and took them out of the monastery courtyard again.

She heard voices below and, looking down the hill towards the cluster of houses, saw Kassa and Petros squatting together on a patch of bare ground. The bags from the packhorse were beside them.

The sun was going down fast now. It was lighting the sky in a blaze of red and orange. In spite of herself, she had to admit that this was one of the most beautiful places she had ever seen. The hillside dropped steeply away below the little hamlet, and beyond it a vista of craggy mountains swept into the distance for what seemed like hundreds of miles. In the evening light their soaring cliffs glowed pink and orange, while the abysses below were a rich, dark purple. Not far away, standing in a gap in a brushwood fence that surrounded a hut, a couple of women and a group of children were staring at her and smiling.

She waved at them.

Tom ran out of the monastery after her.

'Prof says we can start putting up the tent,' he said. 'Do you know how to do it?'

Once again, his carefree confidence infected her.

This is just a little setback, she thought. That's all it is. A little problem. Just so I wasn't going to think it was too easy.

'Sure I can pitch a tent,' she said, forcing herself to sound cheerful. 'You're looking at the champion tent-raiser of the Horn of Africa.'

Kassa had already started opening the bundle of canvas and poles. The three of them stood and looked down at it all.

'OK,' said Afra, managing a grin. 'So I haven't the least idea how to do this. Come on, you two brain merchants, it's over to you.'

Tom had picked up a pole and was turning it over and over, looking first at one end then at the other, while Kassa was examining the tent pegs. Petros laughed and stood up.

'Afra, take this,' he said, handing Afra a rope. 'And Tom, this.'

A few minutes later, the tent was up.

Tom looked at it doubtfully.

'It doesn't look big enough for five of us,' he said.

'Five? There will only be three,' said Kassa. 'My father's friend lives here. It is his compound where we have put the mules. We will stay with him in his house.'

It wasn't until Prof had opened the food bag

and lit a fire, and was stirring something in the billycan that smelt absolutely delicious, that Afra realized how hungry she was. The sun had set now, and only a faint glow in the far horizon showed where it had gone. The hot, filling plateful of tasty bean stew had lifted Afra's spirits again. Anything seemed possible now.

When the last morsel had been scraped off her dish, she looked up at the few stars that were already glinting against the dark blue velvet sky. The air was cold now, but the fire's red heart glowed deep and warm. Wusha lay beside it, replete and content, his nose resting on his big forepaws. Murmured voices came from the huts nearby, and a faint chanting from within the monastery walls. In all the vast country spreading away below them, there was not a single pinprick of light. It was as if there were no other human beings for hundreds of miles around.

She leant against Prof's arm and sighed.

'This is just the most amazing place I've ever been in my whole life,' she said.

'You know,' said Prof, 'I think that goes for me too.'

'And me,' said Tom. 'What are we going to do tomorrow?'

Prof cleared his throat.

'I thought I might take a look at the monastery with Taddesse,' he said. 'There are one or two interesting archaeological points he said he'd like to discuss with me.'

He sounded so guilty that Tom burst out laughing and even Afra smiled.

'I know what I'd like to do,' said Tom. 'I'd like to go back up to the top and look for the wolves again.'

Afra sat up and looked at him with glowing eyes. She had forgotten about the wolves but now the idea of them seemed to strike a new chord. Suddenly, she longed to see them again. The feeling was so strong that it took her by surprise. It was as if the wolves held a meaning for her, which she could not yet understand.

'That's it, Tom!' she said. 'That's what we'll do. And we'll ask Petros if Kassa can come too.'

10

DANGEROUS DOGS

Afra lay motionless on her back, staring up at the roof of the tent. Moonlight shone weakly through the yellow material, casting a lurid glow over everything. She could make out Prof's still form by the door, and the lumpy outline of Tom's sleeping bag next to hers. Wusha lay snuggled up between them, snuffling from time to time under the influence of a doggy dream.

She couldn't sleep. It was freezing for one thing, and although her sleeping bag was thick her feet felt dead and clammy with cold. Her mind was racing too.

Perhaps I'll never find them, she thought. Perhaps this is all a crazy dream, and Prof's right. Perhaps I ought to accept that they're just not there any more, and I'll never know any more about her or have a real family at all.

She breathed in sharply and let out a heavy sigh. An answering rustle came from Tom's sleeping bag.

'Are you awake?' he whispered.

'Yeah. I can't get to sleep.'

'Me too. I'm frozen. It's like the polar ice cap

in here. I've tried imagining I'm in the Sahara desert and it's boiling, boiling hot but it doesn't do any good.'

'It's a good idea, though. I'll give it a try,' said Afra, trying to shake off her depression.

She shut her eyes and tried to see miles of blistering yellow sand and feel blazing heat on her skin. She managed to summon up a faint glow but it faded almost at once.

'I see what you mean. It doesn't work,' she said. 'How about we're sitting beside this really enormous fire, and it's practically burning us, and there's these beautiful orange flames shooting out all over the place.'

There was silence for a moment as they both tried it out. Almost at once, Afra's mind began to wander.

'Tom,' she said in an even quieter whisper, 'what am I going to do if Giorgis doesn't have any other ideas?'

He didn't answer.

'Did you hear me?' she said.

He grunted.

'Yes. I'm thinking. They came from round here, didn't they, your mum's family?'

'Yes. From round Lalibela, anyway.'

'Then maybe you could get everyone DNA tested to see if they're related to you.'

She snorted too loudly, then lifted her head to see if Prof had moved. He hadn't.

97

'That is just the dumbest idea, Tom. Who's going to pay for it? And anyway, no one would agree. They'd think we were witch doctors or the police or spies or something.'

'OK.' Tom sounded huffy. 'I was only trying to help.'

There was a short silence.

'I'm sorry,' said Afra. 'I didn't mean to bite your head off. It would be a really cool idea if it was a bit more practical.'

Tom yawned and rolled over. His outstretched hand tapped against Wusha and the puppy woke up and began to yelp.

An answering growl came from a nearby dog outside the tent. Wusha jumped to his feet and Afra could feel his little body quivering as he began to bark at the top of his shrill voice. Afra picked him up, trying to calm him.

'Hush, Wusha, quiet now,' she said, looking nervously towards the bumpy outline of Prof's sleeping bag.

The dog was closer now. It was baying at full voice right outside the tent. From some distance away another joined in, and then another.

'Do you think they're trying to get him?' said Afra. 'They wouldn't hurt him, would they? He's just a little puppy, like their own ones.'

'I don't know,' said Tom uncertainly. 'I don't know too much about Ethiopian dogs.'

The animal was so close now that Afra could

see the bulge where its nose was pressing against the tent wall. She sat up, half expecting the thin cloth to be torn in half and a fierce face with gaping jaws to appear in the hole.

Then, in the distance, she heard an eerie whooping cry that filled her with familiar dread.

'Hyenas! That's all we need,' muttered Tom.

Afra was holding Wusha tightly in her arms but the puppy was straining to get away from her.

'I can't hold him, Tom,' she said desperately. 'And Prof hasn't quite shut the tent flap. What if he gets out?'

Before Tom could answer, the cacophony of barking outside stopped abruptly, and a moment later a kind of unearthly howling came from some way away. Wusha seemed to relax in Afra's arms.

'What happened?' she whispered. 'Did they go?'

'Maybe they went off after the hyenas,' said Tom.

'Yes, of course. That's it. Dogs do chase hyenas.'

Wusha had wriggled free at last and was settling back in his old place between them.

Tom yawned.

'That's funny,' he said. 'I'm not cold any more. I'm all warmed up.'

Afra tested her feet against each other.

'Me too,' she said. 'Great. Maybe we can get some sleep now.' Something occurred to her. 'I didn't know you had a thing about heights,' she said. 'You were brilliant on the scary bits. My knees were like little blobs of jelly too.'

Tom didn't answer, and she knew by his steady breathing that he had suddenly fallen asleep.

Prof had already got up when Afra woke the next morning. She could hear his deep voice and Taddesse's lighter, hoarser one. Only a few words were distinguishable.

'Bracket capitals . . .' she heard Prof say. 'Blind arcading . . . central nave . . .'

They're at it already, she thought with disgust. He's obsessed. That's all we'll see of him for the rest of the day.

Tom had got up too. His sleeping bag was empty and rumpled. She looked round for Wusha, but he wasn't there either.

She scrambled into her clothes and went outside. The air was still very cold, though the sun, already well up, was deliciously warm on her skin.

Prof had got the fire going again and a thin column of smoke was rising into the cold crisp air, which was so clear that the horizon, hundreds of miles in the distance, seemed no further than a giant's bound away. The land, which last night had glowed so warmly in the setting sun, sparkled now in a glitter of silver and green. From the village the quiet domestic noises of clinking cooking pots and murmured voices resonated through the stillness.

Prof and Taddesse were sitting beside the fire on a couple of stones, feeding it with sticks to make the kettle boil. Prof looked round and saw her.

'At last!' he said. 'I was afraid you'd sleep all day. Come and have some breakfast. There's bread and jelly and a hard-boiled egg if you want one. There'll be tea too, as soon as we get this darned water to boil.'

'Where's Wusha?' asked Afra.

'He's right here,' said Prof a little shamefacedly.

Afra looked over his shoulder. The puppy was lying on his back on Prof's lap, gazing blissfully up at him while Prof tickled his tummy with a large gentle forefinger.

'I've removed four fleas so far from this puppy of yours,' said Prof, trying to sound stern, 'and if any others have hopped onto me, I'm warning you, I shall be most displeased. Also, he ate most of my breakfast.'

Afra grinned at him.

'You can't fool me, Prof,' she said. 'You're a sucker for him. Same as me.'

A sound from below caught their attention. Two of the big yellow village dogs were fighting. A woman came out of one of the huts and lifted her stick towards them. The dogs slunk away.

Tom and Kassa came running up the slope towards them.

'Is the tea ready yet?' panted Tom. 'And can I have some more breakfast? I'm starving.'

Prof put Wusha down on the ground. The kettle had begun to boil. Afra picked up an egg and began to peel it. Tom spread margarine out of a tin onto a rather stale roll.

'You want some, Kassa?' he said, holding out the bread.

Kassa shook his head.

'Today is Friday, a fasting day for Ethiopians,' he said. 'I cannot eat meat or eggs or butter or anything from animals.'

Tom's eyebrows shot up until they were lost under the thick hair that fell over his forehead. He was about to ask Kassa a question when Afra said sharply, 'Where's Wusha got to?'

They all looked round. Afra saw him first and caught her breath.

Wusha, running off to explore, had tumbled down the steep slope towards the nearest hut. One of the big dogs was standing in front of him, looking down at him and slowly wagging his tail. Wusha, his head raised hopefully, was wagging his own tail so hard that the back half of his whole body wagged too.

Afra let out her breath with relief.

'It's OK,' she said. 'I was worried there for a moment. Hey, Prof, where are you going?'

Prof had already bounded halfway down the slope. He waved his arms threateningly at the big dog, who barked and backed away. Prof scooped up the puppy and came back up the slope with him.

'Did you think they were going to attack him?' said Tom, puzzled. 'I thought they were making friends.'

'Maybe they were,' said Prof grimly. 'But keep him away from them, anyway. Village dogs in Ethiopia haven't been inoculated. He could easily get canine distemper, or something even worse.'

'Canine distemper?' said Tom. 'What does that do?'

'It's a killer,' said Prof. 'I had a dog once, and he was so sick. It was terrible to see him.'

'Wasn't that Benjy?' said Afra. 'Aunt Tidey told me about him. He died, didn't he?'

'Yes, he died,' said Prof.

The kettle had boiled at last. Prof made the tea and handed a mug to Kassa. Kassa looked down into it, saw that there was no milk in it, and accepted it with a smile.

'It is not only canine distemper,' he said. 'There is sometimes rabies too.'

Afra shuddered. She'd seen a dog with rabies once, in Kenya. Saliva had drooled from its mouth and it had walked with a swaying, stumbling gait. Suddenly, in a rage of madness, it had rushed at another dog and bitten it deeply in the neck. A terrified farmer had shot them both.

'Humans can catch rabies, can't they?' said Tom.

'Yes,' said Afra. 'And once you've got it, that's it. You just go crazy and die.'

'You mean there's no cure?' said Tom, looking warily at the dogs below.

'If you get bitten and you get to a doctor quickly, you can get a jab that'll stop the disease in its tracks. But you have to get it quickly. After a day or two it won't save you,' said Prof.

'There was very bad rabies here two years ago,' said Kassa, gingerly sipping his hot tea. 'Some dogs, they followed the shepherds up on top.' He indicated with his chin the cliff above the monastery and the plateau beyond it. 'The dogs, they liked to play with the wolves, and to chase them. The wolves became infected with rabies. Half of them died.'

'But that's terrible!' said Tom. 'I mean, there are hardly any wolves left anyway.'

'Yes.' Kassa nodded. 'Here, maybe, in all these mountains, there are only a hundred. The dog, he is a big enemy for the wolf, although he wants to be his friend.'

'You hear that, Wusha?' said Prof, scratching the puppy under his ear. 'You stay away from wolves, OK?' Wusha yawned happily and tried to lick Prof's finger. 'This puppy is a real comeback kid,' said Prof admiringly. 'Look at him. A couple of days of good food and proper care and he's a regular little dog instead of a sorry little bag of bones.'

'Could he have caught anything from those dogs down there?' Afra said, anxiously eyeing the village dogs, who had flopped down by the door of one of the huts.

'I guess not,' said Prof. 'They didn't actually touch each other. I don't think so, anyway.'

Tom jumped up.

'Come on,' he said. 'I'm dying to get back up there and explore. I even feel strong enough to tackle that cliff again.'

'Me too,' said Afra. 'But maybe I ought to stay with Wusha.' She looked at Prof. 'Unless— Hey, Prof, couldn't you . . .?'

Prof shook his head.

'Sorry,' he said. 'I'm going to be in the monastery all morning with Taddesse. And anyway, he's safer with you. The dogs here are just a little too interested in him. Take plenty for him to eat, and keep him away from the wolves. Oh, and don't lose him up there. I don't want to have to spend days and days trying to track him down!'

11

THE PUPS AT THE DEN

Wusha seemed quite happy to curl up in the rucksack again. His energetic early start had tired him out already, and, like a baby, he was ready for his morning nap. Afra had packed the bottom of the rucksack with his bowl, a bottle of water, food for him, and snacks for the three of them. She'd covered it all with a sheet of plastic and spread his towel on top. She'd pulled the cover half over, to give him shade, but had left a good crack through which he could gaze out at the world when he woke up.

She was ready at last and looked round for the others. Prof and Taddesse were already up beside the monastery, talking to the monk in the yellow robe. Tom and Kassa were nowhere to be seen.

Afra frowned. A little feeling of – not exactly jealousy, more the threat of jealousy – was beginning to creep over her. Tom and Kassa had made friends at once. They kept doing things together. They'd spent an hour after breakfast trying to divert a marching line of ants, which had worn, with their tiny feet, a miniature sunken highway across the hard ground. Tom had been telling

Kassa about the leading stars in the Kenya national football team, and kept trying to imitate the way Kassa carried his stick across the back of his shoulders, resting his wrists on it so that his hands dangled down on a level with his ears. Kassa kept asking Tom eager questions about England.

But I'm the Ethiopian one, Afra thought. He ought to be my friend really.

She could hear them now, coming up from the house below, where Petros and Kassa had spent the night.

'What?' Kassa was saying. 'You mean in England the sun is not going down at the same time every day?'

'No, I told you,' Tom said. 'In the summer it doesn't get dark till nine o'clock or even later. We went on holiday in Scotland once, and you could sit outside and play cards until eleven o'clock at night.'

Kassa looked incredulous.

'And,' Tom went on, enjoying the sensation he was creating, 'in the winter it's totally dark and creepy at half past four in the afternoon.'

'Where have you been?' Afra called out, an edge of irritation in her voice. 'Are you coming or not?'

'Oh sorry,' said Tom. 'Kassa's been getting me this brilliant stick. Look, it's like his.' He lifted the stick and laid it over his shoulders behind his head, draping his arms over it. 'Ow! I'm so stiff! I haven't got over all that riding yesterday.'

'Ethiopia would toughen you up if you stayed here,' said Afra. 'You have to be real hard to be an Ethiopian.'

She was rewarded with a smile from Kassa.

'It is true,' he said, flexing his muscles. 'Ethiopian people, they are very strong and brave. Very *gobez*.'

Tom had already set off towards the cliff.

'I'll show you how *gobez* I am then,' he said. 'English people are just as good as you lot.'

Afra rolled her eyes.

Why do boys go in for all these silly competitions all the time? she thought. Tom and Joseph are just the same at home.

The steep climb seemed shorter and easier than it had the night before, but even so it was half an hour before Afra reached the top. The boys had raced up at scrambling speed. Afra, weighed down by the rucksack and mindful of the sleeping Wusha, was forced to go up more slowly.

Tom and Kassa had flopped down onto the short tussocky grass.

'Hey,' said Tom, looking contrite. 'I'd forgotten you had all that on your back. I'll take it if you like.'

Afra shook her head. She was hot and breathless from the climb.

'It's OK. He's asleep. He'd wake up if I took

the rucksack off.' She was looking round already, half expecting a wolf to appear straight away. 'Which way should we go, Kassa? Back along the track where we saw them yesterday?'

Kassa wrinkled his nose thoughtfully as he scanned the plateau. It sloped up gently through a mass of scrubby bushes, hung with grey-green lichens, towards barer ground above.

'They are not always in the same place,' he said. 'Every day they go in a different way, to find new foodstuffs. They will not be here, but up there, where there are no bushes and the earth is soft. That is a good place for them. Their food is small rodent animals, like the mole rat.'

'The what?' said Tom.

'The mole rat. It is a furry animal, very long. It is only here in Ethiopia. You will not find it in other countries.'

'Like the wolf,' said Afra.

'Yes. The wolf, they are special only for Ethiopians.'

Afra smiled at him.

That includes me, she thought.

'That's so stupid,' said Tom discontentedly. 'Animals don't belong to anyone. They're themselves. I mean they sort of belong to the world.'

'Yeah, I guess,' said Afra unwillingly. She'd felt a strong tug from her Ethiopian side and now Tom was dragging her back to her other self again.

Kassa had already set off at speed up the track and was far above them. Afra shivered. Now that the heat of the climb had worn off, the biting wind was beginning to chill her. A faint mewing came from overhead and she looked up. A pair of great buzzards was circling on lazy wings overhead.

'Tom, can you check on Wusha?' she said, suddenly anxious. 'I can't see him unless I take this thing off.'

Tom peeked in under the rucksack cover.

'Totally crashed out,' he said.

Kassa was waiting for them further up the path. Small puffy clouds, scudding fast and low across the sky, were casting shifting shadows on the ground so that Kassa's tall, still figure in his red sweatshirt almost seemed to flicker in the alternating light and shade.

'How does he do it?' panted Tom. 'How does he go so fast? I'm puffed out already.'

'It's the altitude, I guess,' said Afra, who was breathless too. 'He must be used to it.'

They reached Kassa at last. He shaded his eyes against the sun and pointed down into the dip below.

'It is a good place for them here,' he said.

'How do you know?' asked Tom.

'The earth, you can see it? They have been digging in it for their hunting,' answered Kassa, peering down through narrowed eyes.

Afra could see what he meant. Even from up here it was clear that the soft ground was pitted and scarred with holes and little mounds of freshly excavated earth. She looked round eagerly. Nothing stirred in the great sweep of land beyond them except for a flock of twittering siskins. She was disappointed. It had been so easy yesterday. They'd seen two wolves without even trying. She'd expected to come upon them straight away today.

Kassa set off again, down into the hollow. The earth was soft underfoot, spongy from the night ice which had just melted in the heat of the rising sun. They peered down into the holes which dotted the surface, but their shy occupants had either been hunted out or had retreated deep underground.

'Look! Over there!' said Tom, pointing excitedly to the horizon. 'Oh, I thought it was a wolf but it's just a bush or a rock or something.'

It was the first of many disappointments. They wandered aimlessly over the rough terrain, sometimes climbing up clumps of tumbled boulders, sometimes running down to look for fresh tracks by ponds that had formed in the hollows. Once or twice, thinking they were lost, Tom or Afra looked round anxiously for familiar landmarks, but Kassa simply shrugged when they questioned him, and indicated the way home by briefly lifting his head and pointing his chin.

They stopped at last, hungry and thirsty, and took refuge from the freezing wind behind a ridge of rocks.

'It's no good,' said Tom despondently. 'They're just not around. I can't believe it – when we saw them twice yesterday!'

'But we were so lucky,' said Kassa. 'They are very rare. In all of these mountains you can only find maximum a hundred. But I think perhaps we can be lucky again. We know they are here somewhere, and when you have seen one, you have a good chance to see more, because they will not move far from the hunting ground they have chosen. Also, because it is a pack, when you see one, others will not be far away.'

'They must be somewhere close, though,' said Tom. 'I mean those holes we passed just now look really fresh.'

Afra said nothing. She had taken a now restless Wusha out of the rucksack and set him down on the ground. Tom had dug below Wusha's towel to retrieve the food, and now he handed round bread rolls and biscuits. The boys were tucking into theirs, but Afra sat with her own untasted in her hand, looking out across the bare plateau.

Depression was settling on her again, a lowering sense of failure. She'd been so sure, so certain, that she'd find her mother's family here in Ethiopia, but the chances were receding now, further and further into the realms of the impossible.

She'd caught thrilling glimpses, as if a curtain had momentarily billowed out in the wind, when Giorgis had talked of her mother and Taddesse had spoken about Seyoum. But they'd been agonizingly fleeting, tantalizingly insubstantial. They'd whetted her appetite and left her in painful suspense.

'We've come all this way,' said Tom, echoing her thoughts, 'and we haven't even seen a wolf's whisker.'

Afra remembered the roll in her hand and bit down into it.

That's it, she thought. If we don't see any wolves today it'll be like a sign or something. I'll ust give up. But if we do, I'll know I'm still in with a chance of finding my family . . .

She didn't dare finish the thought.

Tom was passing round the bottle of water. Kassa took it and drank delicately, holding it above his mouth so that his lips didn't touch the plastic rim. Tom watched admiringly and tried to do the same, but he tipped it too far and water splashed down his front.

'Aaghh!' he spluttered. 'It's freezing!'

They all laughed.

Afra began packing the remains of the picnic away, while Kassa retrieved Wusha, who had been investigating a mole rat hole. Clouds had covered the sky, and now that the sun was veiled they were beginning to feel the cold.

'It will rain, I think,' said Kassa, pushing his hands deep into his trouser pockets. 'It is better to go back.'

'Not yet!' said Afra sharply. 'Please, let's go on a bit further.'

She couldn't explain the link in her mind between the hunt for wolves and the quest for her family.

Kassa smiled a little distantly and they both looked at Tom.

'We could go a bit further,' he said doubtfully, not wanting to be the one to make the decision. 'Just up to those rocks maybe. Then we'd better go back like Kassa said. It wouldn't be great going down the cliff in a storm.'

Kassa had settled Wusha back in the rucksack and was already hoisting it up onto his back.

'It is my turn,' he said firmly to Afra.

She didn't argue. The rucksack had begun to feel heavy. It was good to be free of it now.

She ran ahead of the others and was the first to reach the rocks. She scrambled up to the top of them and looked down into the dip below.

She was looking straight ahead at first and didn't see anything except for another shallow dip of land, rising to another low rocky outcrop beyond. Then a movement caught her eyes and, looking to her left, she saw something that took her breath away.

A hole had been dug out on the opposite slope and a wolf was lying in the entrance way. It was a female, smaller and paler than the one Afra had seen the day before. Her ears were pricked and her eyes watchful. In front of her, not too far from the mouth of the den, four pups were romping, tussling, rolling about and falling over each other. Their fur, already thick, was a soft dusky brown. Their fluffy bodies were plump and healthy, and their black tails, furred to the tip, curled and wagged as they played.

Afra slid back down the boulder and signalled to the others. They crept forward stealthily and, a moment later, their three heads rose with infinite caution above the rocks. The adult seemed uneasy. She lifted her head and sniffed, making small whining noises in her throat. A minute later, from the rocks behind, another wolf appeared.

It's the one we saw yesterday, thought Afra. With the kink in her tail.

The pups yelped and trampled over themselves, racing towards her. The female lowered her nose to each of theirs in turn.

It's almost like she's kissing them, thought Afra.

Then, jostling each other, they pushed their way round the female's side and snuffled their noses into the soft white fur of her belly, looking for her teats. She stood still to allow them to drink.

The smaller female stood up, stretched, yawned, and trotted away.

It's incredible. She's sort of like, well, almost like a babysitter, thought Afra.

A sunburst of joy flooded her head.

'We saw them! We found them!' she breathed.

Her quest was on again.

12

WOLF SONG AT DAWN

'I don't understand why there are hardly any wolves left,' said Tom as they trudged back down towards the monastery an hour later. Luckily, the massive rain clouds sweeping over the plateau had passed them by, and they'd only been splattered by a few heavy drops. 'I mean, they haven't got any real enemies, have they? Leopards, or lions or anything. Except for dogs and their diseases.'

'It's the habitat, I suppose,' said Afra. 'They probably don't like being too near people, and people are everywhere now.'

'Good thing people don't go up on the top there much then,' said Tom.

'But they do,' objected Kassa. 'Even if there is not so much for goats and sheep to eat, the boys bring them up here for pasture when there is no rain anywhere and the grass below has been eaten.'

'And the dogs come up with them, I suppose,' said Tom.

'Yes, and the boys, they will chase the wolf with sticks and stones because they are afraid.'

'I thought you said the farmers like them because they keep jackals away?' said Afra.

'But the boys, they do not know this. They like to throw stones when they see a wild animal.'

They were approaching the doorway into the monastery. Prof and Taddesse were standing just inside it, talking to a priest.

'There you are!' said Prof, sounding relieved. 'I was afraid you'd been caught in the rain.' He went round behind Kassa who was still carrying the rucksack, lifted the flap and looked in. 'Dead to the world,' he said. 'Sleeping like a baby. Did you see any wolves?'

'Wow, did we ever!' and 'You bet!' said Tom and Afra together.

'And they were outside their den place, like a little cave they'd dug out, and there were four pups. We watched them playing. It was brilliant,' said Tom.

'Really?' Prof's eyebrows shot up in amazement. 'Watching young wolves at play, that's a rare treat. I wish I'd seen them.'

'You can!' said Afra eagerly. 'On the way back to Lalibela. The place isn't far off the track.'

He smiled at her.

'I'd really like that. You're sure we won't distress them by being there?'

'No.' She tucked her hand into his. 'There's this great place to watch them from. I don't think they knew we were there at all.'

'Wow,' said Tom. 'I've just thought of something. We've seen seven wolves altogether. So if there are five hundred wolves alive, that means 1.4 per cent of the whole world population.'

Afra was impressed.

'You're an egghead, Tom, you know that? You do math like that in your head for fun?'

'Sometimes.' Tom tried to look modest.

'There's something I'd like to show you, too,' said Prof, who had been saying something to the priests in Amharic. 'It's in the monastery.'

Afra looked at him warily. She'd been dragged round too many ancient sites while Prof enthused over rows of old stones.

He saw the look on her face and laughed.

'No, really, you'll like this. I know you will. Kassa, have you been into this monastery before?'

Kassa nodded.

'Yes. So many times.'

'Then will you look after Wusha for us? You will? OK, kids. Come with me.'

Afra and Tom followed him into the courtyard. The priest smiled and nodded. Taddesse appeared at the door of the church.

'Do you have the flashlight?' Prof called out to him.

Taddesse held the torch out and stood aside while Prof, Tom and Afra kicked off their shoes and went into the church.

It took Afra a moment to get used to the dim

smoky interior. Then Prof switched on the torch and shone it round the walls. Tom and Afra jumped back in amazement. Figures of saints and angels, of kings on thrones and warriors on prancing horses seemed to surge out from the golden-painted walls in brilliant reds and greens and blues. Neat caps of black hair crowned their heads, and their eyes, under high arched brows, were so alive they seemed to stare out as if from the faces of living souls.

'Look,' said Tom, his voice squeaky with astonishment. 'That one on a horse, spearing that snake or whatever it is. It's like George and the dragon.'

'It is George and the dragon,' said Prof. 'He's just as famous here as he is in Europe.'

'And there's the Virgin Mary with Jesus on her lap,' said Afra. 'She's so calm and kind of solemn. An Ethiopian Mary! Hey, look at that little devil up there in the corner, with horns and an arrow on the end of his tail.'

'Here's a funny one,' said Tom, his eyes following round the wall with the beam of the torch. 'Who's the guy standing on one leg? And oh! Ugh! The other leg's on the floor, look, with a bloody stump.'

Taddesse had followed them in.

'St Tekle Haimanot,' he said. 'He was a great saint for Ethiopia. He was so holy, he stood on one leg for seven years while he prayed. The other leg died and fell off him.'

'Weird,' said Tom enthusiastically. 'This is amazing, this place. Who did it? Who painted it?'

'Who knows?' said Prof. 'These frescoes are hundreds of years old. There are others like this all over Ethiopia. It's a totally unique kind of art.'

They stumbled out into the daylight again.

'That was wonderful,' said Afra, shading her eyes from the sudden intense light. She saw Tom looking at her critically. 'What's got into you?'

'I've just noticed something,' he said. 'You look like those faces in there. Your forehead's kind of round, and you've got those sort of half moon eyebrows.'

Afra flushed with pleasure.

'Wow. That's the best compliment anyone ever paid me.'

'I don't mean you're beautiful or anything,' said Tom, revolted at the thought of paying compliments. 'It's just that . . .'

'It's OK, don't spoil it,' she said, laughing. 'Let's go down to the tent and get something to eat. I'm starving.'

Petros was squatting near the tent, talking to two other men from the little village. He looked up when he heard them coming. He said something to Kassa in Amharic and Kassa briefly answered him. He had taken the rucksack off, and Afra took Wusha out and put him down on the ground. Petros turned to Tom.

'You saw wolf with babies? That is good.'

'Yeah. There were four,' Tom began eagerly. 'And they had this den, and—'

A bark interrupted him, and a village dog, seeing Wusha, came slinking forward. One of the farmers picked up a pebble, and the dog, reading the signal correctly, retreated towards the fence of the nearest compound where another dog was standing in the shade.

Something about the tense way the dog in the shade was holding itself caught Afra's attention.

'Hey, that dog doesn't look too good,' she said.

Even from this distance she could see that it was trembling and that its eyes were wild and staring.

She went towards it.

'Afra, it is better to leave him!' Petros called out urgently. 'The dog is sick.'

'What's the matter with him?' she asked.

He shrugged.

'I do not know. They have tied him to keep him from running about.'

'You don't think . . . He doesn't have rabies, does he?'

'I do not think so. I do not know. He has a fever only, maybe.'

Afra shivered and looked down at Wusha, who was earnestly engaged in a fight to the death with the trailing end of one of the tent's guy ropes.

'I'm not letting you out of my sight,' she murmured grimly.

The evening passed slowly. They lit the fire again, and Prof brewed up a hot supper out of a whole lot of tins, and Wusha ate and played and ate again, and everyone else ate their supper ravenously too. Then, as the sky darkened and the stars came out one by one, they wrapped themselves in their sleeping bags and huddled by the fire, Taddesse, Kassa and Petros looking like large substantial ghosts in their cosy white *shamma*s. Then Prof and Taddesse began to tell legends of old Ethiopia, stories of archangels and emperors, of miracles and mysteries.

'That's enough!' Prof said at last, noticing that Tom's eyelids were sinking lower and lower. 'Bed.'

Afra fell asleep as soon as she had snuggled down into her sleeping bag, in spite of the cold and the hard ground underneath her. Prof had carefully closed the bottom flap of the tent so that Wusha couldn't get out, and if dogs or hyenas were baying outside she never heard them.

She woke early and looked at her watch. The others were still asleep. It was barely six o'clock. Dim daylight penetrated the yellow walls of the tent but the sun had obviously not yet risen. She lay still for a moment, wondering what had woken her. A strange sound still lingered on the edge of her consciousness, but she couldn't think what it had been.

Then it came again. It was a wild chorus of howls, from high up and far away, carrying clearly on the still dawn air from the freezing windy wilderness above. Voice after voice joined in, rising one above the other, pouring out into the cold morning the ancient, beautiful wolf song.

Every nerve in Afra's body quivered in response. She had never heard anything like this in her whole life before, and she knew she never would again.

13
RABIES!

It wasn't until they'd almost finished breakfast and Prof was blowing on the embers of the fire to get the kettle to boil again for a second round of tea, that Afra noticed something.

'That sick dog,' she said. 'It's gone.'

Everyone looked down towards the bare patch by the brushwood fence where the dog had been lying the day before.

'Maybe it's better and they let it go,' said Tom.

Petros was coming up from his friend's house below, where he and Kassa had spent the night. He ducked his head politely to everyone in turn and began on the long ritual of Amharic morning greetings with Prof.

I'd never be able to learn this language, thought Afra, listening admiringly. I could never make all those kinds of explosion noises.

It was rude, she knew, to interrupt the greeting, so she waited as patiently as she could, and as soon as it was over she said, 'Ato Petros, do you know what happened to that dog? The one who was sick last night?'

Petros settled himself in a comfortable squat

near the fire and rearranged the *shamma* round his shoulders.

'It was not good,' he said. 'This dog, he became mad in the night. He was too strong. He bit his rope and escaped.'

'Then it is rabies,' said Prof, looking grave.

'Rabies, yes.' Petros nodded. 'It is better to be careful if he approaches near us.'

Prof was looking worried.

'Right,' he said. 'We need to make a start, and I think it ought to be as soon as possible. With a rabid dog on the loose . . . Petros, which way did it go?'

Petros lifted his chin towards the horizon.

'They say it went down there. Into the valley.'

'How far is the nearest village?' asked Prof.

'They have a sent a boy to warn them.' Petros understood the meaning of Prof's question. 'There has been rabies here before, many times. The people, they know what to do.'

'But the wolves!' Afra's voice rose sharply with anxiety. 'What if a dog gets up there and spreads it to them?'

She looked round quickly for Wusha, who, fascinated by a butterfly, was making little snapping leaps towards the bush where it was perching.

'We'll contact the conservation authorities and see if they can send out a team as soon as we get back to Lalibela,' said Prof, standing up and beginning to clear away the breakfast dishes. 'Give me a hand with these, Afra.'

From the valley below came a sudden hysterical burst of barking. Prof hesitated, then seemed to make up his mind.

'No, we can't risk it. Afra, Tom and Kassa . . . Where is Kassa, by the way?'

'He is preparing the horses,' said Petros. 'He will come now.'

'Good. Afra and Tom, get back into the tent and pack up your stuff. When Kassa gets here, you can take two of the mules and go up on top at once. I don't think a sick dog's very likely to tackle that climb. He's much more likely to circle round and come back home. I have to get you out of the way.'

Afra pursed her lips.

'We're not scared. Anyway, don't you need us to help you with the tent and everything?'

'Petros and I will manage fine,' said Prof. 'It's not only you I'm thinking about. You have to get Wusha out of harm's way.'

'OK, Prof,' said Afra, and dived back into the tent to sort out her things.

'Where will we meet you?' said Tom.

'Good point, Tom. I don't know. On the track somewhere.'

'I know!' said Tom. 'There's a place where the track bends round to the right. We'll leave the mules on the corner, but if you go left there and over the next dip, we'll be a hundred metres or so further on. That's where you can watch the wolves' den from.'

Prof's face lightened.

'Excellent. I'll get the chance to see them too. Go on, now, Tom. I won't be comfortable until you're all safely out of here.'

Afra felt springs in her legs as she climbed up the steep cleft in the rock wall for the last time. The fresh mountain air and the long hours of riding and walking and climbing had made her feel boundingly fit and energetic. She was getting used to the altitude too.

For the time being her worries had receded to a comfortable distance. She'd be certain to find someone, one day, sooner or later, who would tell her about her family. And Prof would weaken over Wusha, she was sure, and let her take him home. He was halfway there already. And the rabid dog was probably miles away by now, being dealt with by some tough experienced Ethiopian farmers.

It was impossible to feel despondent on such a golden morning. The sun was well up now, deliciously warm on her back, dispelling the last pockets of mist that lay in the deep folds between the mountains. A bird piped out his morning song on a rock above, and tiny star-like flowers sprouted from the cliff face. From the monastery below came voices raised in laughter.

She had gone ahead of Tom and Kassa. Prof had almost hustled her away from the campsite. He kept saying testily, 'For heaven's sake, Afra, stop dawdling about. Get going. Get that puppy out of here.'

She'd enjoyed his anxiety. She knew it had really been for her.

The boys were not far behind her. Tom, his precious stick in his hand, his panting breath billowing out in clouds as it condensed in the cold air, was climbing doggedly, concentrating on the steep path, keeping his eyes away from the drop below. Kassa was working furiously hard, urging Mamete up the slope ahead of him with harsh, anxious cries and thumps of his hand on her rump. At the same time he was tugging on the bridle of the second mule, who was less sure-footed than Mamete and in constant danger of slipping.

They burst out at last onto the plateau above. The mules stood for a moment, trembling, shaking their heads so that their bridles jingled.

'Come on,' said Tom eagerly. 'What are we waiting for? Let's go and see if the wolves are still there.'

This end of the vast plateau seemed almost familiar now. They let their mules rest a few moments longer then set off confidently along the path, recognizing rocks and pools of water, anticipating where the sharp bend in the road would be.

'I will stay here with the mules,' Kassa said to Afra when they'd reached the turning. Tom had already started to run as quietly as he could towards the viewing place.

'Let's take it in turns,' said Afra. 'Do you want to go first?'

'No, no, it is all right. You go.' Kassa bent down to adjust Mamete's girth and Afra could see he didn't want to leave his post. She turned to go but Wusha, riding high in the rucksack on her back, was whining and scrabbling at the side of it. He was stronger today and seemed even livelier.

'You can leave him with me,' said Kassa. 'Mamete is used to him now and that other one' – he jerked his head towards the second mule – 'he is not worried about dogs.'

Afra hesitated. Wusha was becoming more and more restless, yapping now, standing on his back legs and threatening to tumble out of the rucksack. In this mood he'd either frighten the wolves away or attract them to come too close.

'All right,' she said reluctantly. 'Thanks. Are you sure you don't mind?'

Kassa had already lifted Wusha down from the rucksack. His tail wagging wildly, the puppy set off purposefully towards a hole in the ground nearby, and began to burrow, shovelling the earth so inexpertly that clumps kept hitting his face.

Afra laughed, then she took off, and a moment later she was crouching beside Tom, looking between the rocks down towards the wolves' den.

For a moment she saw nothing more than the bare dip and the tumbled boulders and clumps of grey-green leaves, and she felt a keen disappointment. Then, looking to her right, she saw the young adult again. The wolf was half concealed by a boulder and had been bending her head to lick her foreleg. She stepped out into the open and yawned, pointing her long narrow snout upwards and momentarily shutting her slanting eyes.

The pups scrambled out after her. At once two of them, the largest, began a play fight, boxing with raised paws and trying to grab with their sharp little teeth the fur on each other's backs. The other two, sitting up on their haunches, watched the fight with interest, turning solemn wide-eyed faces from one to the other.

Then, up on the ridge above the den, a larger wolf appeared. His coat was a dark glowing terra-cotta and his bushy tail was raised in a gesture of supremacy. He stood tall and confident, his head turned away, scanning the landscape in front of him.

Without a word, Tom and Afra sank slowly back behind the rock. They'd been lucky so far. The wind had been in the right direction, coming from the wolves towards them, and the babysitter female and the pups hadn't noticed them. But this magnificent powerful male was another matter. His keen eyes would pick them up easily as soon as he looked this way.

They crouched, motionless, for a few minutes, then, very cautiously, they lifted their heads and looked again. The babysitter and the pups were still there but the male wolf had gone.

At that moment, a faint whinnying noise came from behind her.

Prof and Petros must have come up with the horse and the other mule, thought Afra with satisfaction. Great. I can't wait for Prof to see this.

Tom, aware of a tickling on his ankle, turned round sharply to flick a marauding insect off it. Afra heard him gasp, and his hand closed over her arm in a painful grip.

'Look there! The dog!' he hissed.

Afra whipped round and looked behind her. She recognized the dog at once. She had last seen it standing by the brushwood fence below the campsite, its head lolling forward, shivering. Now the mad creature sent a shudder of pity and horror through her. The dog was limping, its whole body lopsided, its fur puckering in violent convulsions. Its eyes, wide and empty, focused on nothing, and its tongue rolled out of its mouth, from which saliva was dribbling.

'Keep still,' whispered Tom. 'Maybe it'll go right past and won't realize we're here.'

Afra forced herself to stay motionless, willing the wolf pups, who had momentarily relaxed into a soft mound of dark brown fur, to stay quiet.

Then she saw something that made her bite her lip till her teeth nearly cut into it.

Unconcerned, concentrating only on returning to her pups, the female wolf's taut, elegant figure appeared. She was running at an easy trot along the dip below the den. The pups all saw her at the same time and broke into an ecstasy of whines and yelps.

The dog turned its head. Its back was arched now, the rough hair on its neck bristling ferociously. It started to run forward at an awkward sideways trot towards the sound of the pups.

At that moment, another sound made the dog falter in its tracks. Another young creature's sharp, high-pitched barks rang out on the still air. The dog turned its head. Wusha was bouncing and tumbling across the rough ground towards Afra, his pink tongue flapping, his oversized paws splashing in the puddles.

He was running straight into the path of the rabid dog.

14

AN AGONIZING DECISION

Afra leapt to her feet and stood stock still in an agony of indecision. The dog was the scariest thing she had ever seen, more terrifying, more dangerous than a charging rhino or a hunting leopard. Her instincts were screaming at her to run away. But Wusha! And the wolf pups! How could she leave them to their fate? And which should she try to save?

She took a step towards Wusha, then the thought of the wolves tugged her in the opposite direction. Wusha was hers – her puppy, her responsibility, depending on her, trusting her, but the wolves were the last precious remnants of an ancient race. If rabies took hold of them again they would be nudged even closer to their final extinction.

With a sob, she turned her back on Wusha and, jumping over the wall of boulders, she went hurtling down towards the wolves, shouting idiotically, 'Shoo! Go away! Run!'

It had seemed as if she'd been standing still for ages but in fact it had only been for a few seconds.

Behind her she heard Tom let out a wild, hoarse battle-cry.

The adult wolf stood her ground. She snarled and bared her teeth, while the pups scrambled to get into the dark shelter of the den.

'No! No! Don't go in there! Run away! Don't you understand?' cried Afra despairingly.

She looked round. She was in the dip herself now and she could see Tom's upper half above the rocks. He disappeared for a moment, then was up again, with his stick in one hand and Wusha in the other.

Afra raced up towards him, climbing on all fours back up the steep slope to the top of the ridge. She leapt over the crest of boulders.

The mad dog was running straight for Tom, snapping his powerful teeth as he came, trails of saliva drooling from his mouth. Tom, hampered by Wusha, who was struggling in the crook of his left arm, lifted his stick. Afra darted forward to take Wusha from him, and then, so quickly that afterwards she could hardly piece together what had happened, Wusha struggled free and dropped with a screaming yelp to the ground. Tom, aiming for the dog's head, missed and brought the stick down just ahead of it. It snapped in two on a boulder.

The dog lunged forwards, its jaws open, almost choking on its crazed snarl, and its teeth were about to close on Wusha's foreleg when Afra, with a scream of 'No! No!' lunged forward and snatched Wusha to safety.

The dog, leaping up in a frenzy of rage, caught her left hand and bit deeply into it.

Beside her, Tom had picked up the broken halves of his stick and was beating at the dog with them. It dropped away from Afra's hand and rushed at Tom.

Horror and fury possessed Afra. With a snarl almost as vicious as the dog's, she flung Wusha down to the ground, picked up the first thing that came to hand, a big flat stone, and brought it crashing down onto the dog's head. There was a sickening crunch as its skull splintered and then it lay still.

Afra felt the blood drain out of her head. She was weak and dizzy. Blood and saliva dripped from her hand and she stood looking down at it in a daze.

'He bit me,' she said slowly. 'I killed him. I killed an animal.'

She heard Tom beside her taking a shuddering breath, then she stumbled away towards a large boulder and sat down on it. Her stomach heaved and she was violently sick.

When it was over she felt something on her shoe and looking down saw that Wusha was playing his favourite game of chewing at her laces.

I've got rabies. If I don't get help soon I'm

going to go crazy and die, she thought, but she couldn't take it in.

She looked round. Tom had gone. She got to her feet, her head swimming. Where was he? Surely he wouldn't leave her here, all alone?

Then she saw him running towards her and behind him, covering the ground with great bounds of his long legs, was Prof.

'Oh Daddy, Daddy!' she cried, and sitting down on the rock again she burst into tears.

Prof knelt down beside her.

'Did it get you? Where?' he said urgently.

She held out her hand. The blood was still welling out of the puncture marks. There were four of them and two were deep.

'Water. We need soap and water,' muttered Prof. 'We must wash it at once.'

Tom dragged at his arm.

'There's a little pool,' he said, 'just over there. It looks really clean. I'll get my soap from my bag.'

Prof put his arm under Afra's shoulders and half carried her to the pool. She was trying hard to control her sobs but she couldn't stop the violent trembling of her arms and legs. Prof took her arm and plunged her hand down into the icy water. The shock made her cry out, but it cleared some of the faintness from her head. Tom had raced back, the soap in his hand, and Prof worked it gently but ruthlessly into the wound, cleaning it again and again.

'I've got it, rabies, haven't I?' she said, looking up at him.

Prof slipped off his soft cotton scarf and bound it round Afra's hand.

'Even if you're infected, you're going to be all right.' She could see that he was making a super-human effort to stay calm. 'We're going to shoot you so full of antidote you'll be a walking anti-rabies machine.'

'How long have I got? Will they have any stuff in Lalibela?'

'Of course they will.' His voice was hearty.

He's not sure, he's worried too, she thought, fear settling in the pit of her stomach.

Tom was standing anxiously beside them, Wusha in his arms.

'What are we going to do about that?' he said, pointing to the dead dog. 'We shouldn't leave it like that. The wolves might come and eat it.'

Prof looked at the dead dog with disgust.

'I thought they were hunters, not scavengers. The birds will probably deal with it very soon, and they don't get rabies. Look. Here they come already.'

He pointed. A raven was perched on the rock nearby, and another was approaching purpose-fully through the sky.

'Yes, but the wolves might come and sniff at it,' Afra said, 'and get infected that way.'

Prof looked down at his watch, then up again at her.

'You could be right. OK, Tom, quick. Let's get some stones together and pile them on top of it. They'll need to be the biggest ones we can carry so that the wolves can't knock them down. Quick.'

Kassa came running up to them.

'Did something happen?' he said. 'I heard there was some shouts.'

'The mad dog. It was here. It bit Afra. She tried to save the wolves. I hit it and broke my stick, and it went for Wusha, and Afra saved him,' Tom said incoherently.

'It bit Afra?' Kassa stared at her in horror.

She held out her bandaged hand to show him.

'Prof says we can get some antidote in Lalibela.'

'Maybe.' He shook his head doubtfully. 'I do not know.'

'Kassa!' Prof called out angrily. 'Come and help!'

A few minutes later, the dog's body had disappeared under a cairn of heavy stones. Prof picked Wusha up and dumped him back into the rucksack. The puppy was yawning, tired out after the exertions of the morning.

'We've heard enough from you today,' said Prof, dropping the flap down. 'Come on, everyone. Let's get out of here.'

Afra was still feeling dizzy and weak, but she found she could walk now. She was glad, though, of Prof's comforting arm supporting her. Tom walked on the other side of her, carrying Wusha in the rucksack.

'You should have seen her, Prof,' he said. 'She was incredibly brave. She stuck her hand right in front of the dog to get Wusha away from it.'

Afra laughed shakily.

'You were just as bad. Beating at it with your stick.'

'You're both crazy,' said Prof, sounding determinedly cheerful. 'Look, there's Petros with the mules. Not far now.'

Kassa had raced on ahead of them. They could see him now, talking urgently to his father. Then, as they watched, he swung himself into Mamete's saddle and took off at a gallop along the track.

'What's he doing?' said Prof, annoyed. 'Where on earth is he going?'

They came up to Petros. He looked sympathetically at Afra.

'*Aisush!*' he said. She had heard that word before. It meant, 'Be comforted'.

'Kassa has told me,' Petros went on. 'You have been very brave, very *gobez*.'

'Where's the boy gone?' said Prof curtly.

'He is going fast back to Lalibela. Alone with Mamete he can go more fast than us. He will find the clinic and prepare them to receive Afra. And if they have no medicine for rabies, he will ask them to radio Addis Ababa. They will send a supply by Ethiopian Airlines on the next plane.'

'Brilliant,' said Prof, letting his breath out in a gust. 'Petros, that's great. Afra, you'll have to ride my mule this time. Tom and I will take turns to walk.'

Afra laid a trembling hand on the mule's bridle as she prepared to mount. Prof suddenly pulled her into his arms and gave her a fierce hug. Then he held her away from him and looked down searchingly into her eyes.

'You're not to worry about this, do you hear me, honey? You did a great job back there. You've probably saved the lives of countless wolves, never mind that little rascal, Wusha. And I promise you, I *promise* you, that everything's going to be OK. We're going to get that hand to a doctor, and we're going to get you your shots, and you'll never know the difference. Do you believe me?'

She had never seen him look so earnest. She nodded her head.

'I believe you.'

'Good girl. OK, Petros, let's go.'

Petros cupped his hands. Afra put her foot in them and he helped her up into the saddle. Then he patted the mule's rump and it began to walk on. Tom had already mounted the other mule. Prof strode impatiently ahead.

The sky had been brilliantly clear, the blue, deep as stained glass, spreading right down to the horizon, but now a few clouds were coming up, speckling the plateau with patterns of light and shade.

'Look! Afra, there!' Tom shouted from behind her.

Afra looked round at him and followed his pointing arm. The mother wolf was standing on a hillock, silhouetted against the sapphire sky. Her head was turned towards them, her ears sharply pricked, the kink in her tail clearly visible. She was watching them.

Prof had seen her too.

The wolf ducked her head twice, as if in greeting, then, with masterful ease, she turned and walked away, disappearing over the horizon and out of sight.

15

A MEETING AT SUNSET

It was a long seven-hour slog back to Lalibela. Once they were caught in a rain storm and took partial shelter in the lee of a cliff. The rain made Petros mutter and shake his head. It was unseasonal, he said, and would spoil the crops.

Prof walked beside Afra whenever the path was wide enough. Sometimes he talked, sometimes he said nothing. She was happy either way. He was looking after her and she felt comforted.

Her hand throbbed at first, but after a while she didn't feel it so much.

It was mid-afternoon when they came round the last corner and saw the little town of Lalibela, with its labyrinth of trenches and pits, ahead of them. A boy in a red sweatshirt was perched on a rock above the path. He leapt down when he saw them coming.

'Look! There's Kassa!' shouted Tom.

Prof wheeled round.

'Kassa!' he called out. 'Did you get to the clinic?'

Kassa wasn't smiling.

'Yes. It was open, but they do not have any vaccine.'

Afra, who had been lulled into a sense of security by Prof's confident reassurances, felt a jolt of fear that left her legs weak.

'But I have seen Ato Giorgis,' Kassa went on. 'He has radioed to Addis. There is a plane tonight at five o'clock. They will try, they said, to send some vaccine and some antibiotics on it.'

'That's great, Kassa,' said Prof, in the hearty voice that Afra had come to suspect. 'You did a brilliant job. What did you do – sprout wings or something?'

Kassa grinned.

'It was Mamete. She is a very good mule. The best.'

'You should rename her Pegasus,' said Prof.

Kassa looked nonplussed. He had fallen in beside Afra's mule. The fright was fading from her again.

'It's some old horse from a story,' she said apologetically. 'Don't mind Prof. He's always saying things like that.'

They ran into Giorgis in the main open space in the centre of town. He had been talking to a group of *shamma*-clad elders, but he broke away from them and hurried up to the travel-stained cavalcade of mules. There was an anxious crease between his brows.

'Richard!' he called out. 'What's all this I hear?

Rabid dogs? Packs of Simien wolves? I suppose it's all my fault for sending you off on a wild-goose chase.'

He looked at Afra's roughly bandaged hand, which was still resting on the pommel of the saddle, and shook his head, his face grave with sympathy. Then he looked up at her again.

'I don't envy you having injections,' he said, his usual bounciness returning. 'I can't stand the sight of the needle.'

His cheerfulness was infectious and Afra smiled down at him. It felt great to be back in town again. A few days ago, Lalibela had seemed like no more than an overgrown village. Now, fresh from the remote highlands, it seemed like a throbbing metropolis.

She slid off the mule and staggered as she landed. She'd been riding for hours and hours and felt stiff all over.

Giorgis caught her right arm and steadied her.

'Hey! Don't fall. You are a heroine, you know that? You have been saving one of our endemic Ethiopian species.'

Prof looked at him over her head.

'Your message got through, you're sure of it?' he said quietly.

'Yes.' Giorgis dropped his jovial manner. 'They'll do their best. Don't worry, Richard. You have time. If it doesn't come on tonight's plane, it'll be here first thing in the morning. Oh, and by the way, I contacted the wildlife people at the Conservation Bureau. They're going to try to get a rabies inoculation team out here at once. I'm not a wildlife man myself, but everyone seems to think the foxes – or wolves or whatever they are – are just as much a national treasure as our churches and monasteries. These kids deserve a medal. By the way, did you get a chance to see the frescoes? Pretty good, aren't they?'

'Amazing,' said Prof. Afra waited resignedly for him to embark on a discussion of art and archaeology with Giorgis, but instead he said, 'I'll catch up with you later on all that. Right now I have to get this daughter of mine a clean bandage and something to drink. Not to mention the dog.'

The long purple shadows of evening were stretching minute by minute by the time Prof had sorted out everything to his satisfaction. Afra's hand had been carefully washed and disinfected, and a clean bandage, neatly tied, covered the wound. Tom had wolfed down a couple of big bread rolls with a cup of milky coffee. Worku, who had heard by some unknown means the whole story of Tom and Afra's heroic rescue of the puppy and the wolves, had greeted them with open arms and had immediately laid on copious cups of tea and hot water for a wash, while a large bowl of milk and *injera** and chopped liver appeared on the floor of the bar for Wusha.

'How are you feeling, honey?' said Prof at last, when they'd all had a good wash and plenty to drink. 'I guess you need to rest. There's a couple of hours until supper time. Why don't you catch some sleep?'

Afra tested her legs and arms one by one. The wash and the tea had had an amazingly restorative effect, and even her hand hardly hurt at all now unless she touched it.

'I feel fine,' she said, surprised. 'I don't need to rest.'

'Well then,' said Prof. 'Let's go see the most exciting show in town. The sun's going down and the sky will be spectacular. There's a place I know where you can sit and watch it, and it's like seeing a beautiful oil painting come alive as all the colours shift and glow and deepen.'

'What about Wusha?' said Tom, who was tickling the puppy's tummy.

'He's tired.' Prof bent down and picked Wusha up. 'He needs to rest. I'll settle him in our room before we all go out.'

Tom and Afra exchanged grins.

'I don't know what you were worried about,' said Tom. 'He's totally soft on him.'

*A kind of pancake, the main food of Ethiopia

'I know. It's weird.'

Afra looked across to the open door of the room. She could hear Prof's calm, reassuring voice as he arranged Wusha's towel and filled his bowl with water. It was the voice he had used with her when she was little. She felt an unexpected pang of jealousy.

'Maybe he'll make Wusha his own dog,' said Tom, 'and take him on digs and everything. That'd be great.'

'That's stupid,' said Afra sharply. 'He'd never do that.'

But he might, she thought. He really might.

Prof came out and locked the door behind him.

'Good as gold,' he said, looking pleased. 'Yawning his head off. What are we waiting for? Let's go.'

Everyone in Lalibela seemed to have heard about the rabid dog and the wolves, and people stopped to stare and smile and point at Afra's bandaged hand with sharp sympathetic intakes of breath. A crowd of children began to form behind them, which grew and grew until Kassa, suddenly appearing out of nowhere, waved his arms at them indignantly and shooed them away.

They followed Prof back inside the sacred enclosure, but instead of taking them down into one of the deep trenches, he led them out onto a bare hillside.

'There,' he said. 'Look.'

The sun hung low in the sky. The rocks were a deep rose-pink and the shadows a lustrous purple. A few metres away was the lip of a dizzyingly deep pit in which stood a perfect three-storey stone church carved in the shape of a cross. Beyond it the ground swept away to a fringe of trees. Lazy wafts of smoke rose up into the sky from the thatched roofs of a group of round stone huts. Showers of rain drifted like black chiffon veils across the vast panorama of mountains beyond.

Afra sat down on the roots of a gnarled old tree. She felt a kind of nostalgia, a pleasurable sadness.

This is the most beautiful place in the world, she thought, and it's sort of mine, but not mine too because I can't find my family. But I'll always know I belong here, as long as I live.

She wished she hadn't thought that last bit. It reminded her of the bite on her hand. After all, if the vaccine didn't come she mightn't live much longer. The thought was too far-fetched to seem real, but all the same she began to imagine a harrowing deathbed scene. It took hold of her, and soon she was quite unaware of the others.

Tom had asked Prof a question about the church and, delighted by his interest, Prof had moved away with Tom and Kassa and was circling round the edge of the huge pit, pointing things out to them. Afra didn't notice. Anyway, she wanted to be alone.

There were few people about. One or two had walked past since she'd sat down, and a boy had stopped and tried to talk to her, but she hadn't really responded and he'd moved on.

Her sense of sadness was deepening with the gathering darkness into an all-encompassing ache.

'I want my mother,' she whispered.

She thought of all the times she'd needed her, when she'd been little and lonely in the night, when Prof had been away and Sarah had misunderstood her. She thought of secrets she'd never been able to share, and the emptiness where warmth and love should have been. There was a tightness in her throat.

This is silly, she thought severely, and tried to bring herself back from the brink of tears.

A man had been walking briskly up the hill along the path that ran close by. He stopped, out of breath, and looked down at her. She looked up at the same time and met his eye. He had been about to walk on but the intense expression in her face stopped him. He saw her hand and said, 'You have hurt yourself?'

'I was bitten by a dog,' she said reluctantly. She didn't want to go into the whole story with a stranger.

'Oh, you are the one,' he said. 'I heard about it.'

He was staring at her with a slight frown on his face. She looked back at him. He was a startlingly handsome man, tall and slender. His long face was an almost reddish brown, his eyes set wide apart under brows that were arched into a permanently questioning expression. He carried himself stiffly, with a kind of natural arrogance.

'Where are you from?' he said suddenly.

The curtness of his question annoyed her, but she answered, 'From Nairobi.'

'But you're not Kenyan?'

'No.'

He waited, expecting more.

'My father's American,' she said at last. 'My mother is – was – Ethiopian.'

He drew in his breath, and with a sudden folding of his long legs sat down beside her. He was staring at her intently.

He moved back a little, realizing that he might be frightening her, then he smiled and she felt a shiver of recognition. The way his short upper lip stretched across his teeth, his eyes, his long straight nose, even the way the hair grew forwards over his ears, were oddly familiar. She was breathless.

'What's your name?' he said, more gently.

'Afra.'

'No, no.' He was impatient again. 'Your surname. Your whole name.'

'Afra Sablay Tovey.'

Her heart was hammering. She watched his

face melting into disbelief, then into a wild joy. A wonderful hope was blossoming inside her.

'What's your name?' she said.

He laughed unsteadily.

'Don't you know? I'm Seyoum Habtewold, and I'm your uncle.'

She jumped to her feet. She was staring at him as if in a dream. She hardly heard Tom's voice calling from a distance, 'Afra, look! There's the plane! It's coming in to land!'

16

A PRECIOUS PACKAGE

Seyoum was on his feet too. He bent forward and embraced her and she could feel his whole body trembling.

'Afra?' said Prof's chilly voice behind her. 'What's all this? What are you doing?'

She turned round before he had a chance to finish. Her face was blazing so brilliantly that he took a step back.

'It's him! It's Uncle Seyoum!' she cried, shaking her head disbelievingly. 'He found me! I mean we found each other! Just like that.' She turned back to Seyoum. Questions were burning inside her, and she didn't know where to begin. 'When did you come here? Where have you been? How did you *know*?'

Seyoum didn't answer. He was standing still, looking unsmilingly at Prof.

'Richard,' he said with cold formality. 'Welcome to Ethiopia.'

Prof advanced on him, his hands held out, his face beaming.

'Seyoum! I can't believe it! We've been hunting for you everywhere!'

A little of the hardness went out of Seyoum's face.

'You have been hunting for me?'

'Yes! Riding round the country looking for people who might know where you are. A fool's game, I can tell you. This is truly incredible. To run into you, just like that. I'd forgotten of course that Ethiopia is the land of miracles. When I think of all the things I've done to try and trace you . . .'

Seyoum's stance softened further. He was smiling now too.

'Richard, I didn't know of this. We have tried to find you also. I wrote to you many times, but you never replied. I thought maybe – you know – you wished to forget us, or the child had died, or you had a new family—'

'I never got any letters from you!' interrupted Prof. 'If only you knew how I've worried about you! I thought you'd all died in the Red Terror, or the war, or the famine. I've had the most terrible fears – was almost afraid to find out the truth. Where have you been? How did you survive it all? Oh, this is ridiculous! I don't know where to start.'

Afra was looking from one to the other, trying to understand.

'Is that why you kept saying all that about us not ever finding them, Prof?' she said. 'You were scared we'd find out something horrible?'

He put an arm around her shoulders and gave them a squeeze.

'It was.'

Afra was aware now that a small crowd of interested bystanders had gathered. Tom, his mouth open, was in the front row. Kassa was beside him, too enthralled to notice the other children jostling at his elbow.

'I just can't take it all in,' said Afra, whose mind and body were trying to catch up with the rush of emotions threatening to engulf her. 'I mean, why are you here? We thought you were in Germany, or Britain or somewhere.'

'I've come back,' said Seyoum, who seemed almost as overwhelmed. 'I live in Addis now. I work in the Ministry of Education. I come back to Lalibela as often as I can to visit my mother.'

Afra almost staggered.

'Your mother?' she said, and her voice came out squeaky. 'You mean my grandmother? You mean I have a granny here in Lalibela?'

'Yes, of course you have!'

The crowd all around was buzzing now as the news was passed from one to the other. Seyoum became aware of it.

'Richard, I must go and speak to my mother at once,' he said. 'This news will run through the town like a fire. I must see her first, before others go to her and before you come. She is old. She is not so strong now. There will be a shock for her. Come later, after one hour.'

'Where? Where is she?' burst out Afra, who couldn't bear the thought of letting Seyoum out of her sight in case he disappeared again for ever.

Seyoum looked round and saw Kassa. He gave him some rapid instructions in Amharic. The onlookers joined in enthusiastically, and a few runners peeled away from the edge of the crowd, anxious to spread the exciting news.

Seyoum gave Afra another tremendous hug.

'Come later! We – she will be waiting for you,' he cried, and he bounded off on his long legs up the slope towards the town.

When he had gone, Afra turned to Prof and flung her arms around him. She wanted to touch something real and solid to reassure herself that all this hadn't been a dream. He hugged her in return, so hard she was afraid her ribs would crack. Laughing, she pulled herself free.

It was nearly dark now. The crowd was beginning to melt away. Tom and Kassa stood awkwardly nearby, embarrassed by all the emotion. Kassa cleared his throat.

'The Ethiopian Airlines transport,' he said. 'It is coming up from the landing strip. We can meet it now, perhaps?'

'Yes, of course!'

Prof took off his glasses and passed a hand over his eyes.

It's almost as if he was crying, thought Afra wonderingly.

She tucked her hand into his arm and had to restrain herself from skipping like a six-year-old as they walked along behind Tom and Kassa back towards the town.

'I knew it, I knew we'd find him. It was so amazing, such a coincidence. Only it didn't feel like that at all. It felt *meant*. I mean, there I was, sitting on my own, and he kind of came up and saw my bandage and started talking to me, and I even thought, Who is this creep trying to pick me up? And then the way he looked at me was so special, as if he recognized me, and I started recognizing things about him. I mean I really thought I'd seen him somewhere before.'

'You have, in a way,' said Prof. 'You've seen him thousands of times in that photo of your mother.'

'Yes!' she said eagerly. 'He looks just like her. It's weird. His eyes and his nose and the way his hair grows and everything.'

Prof paused for a moment.

'Yes, he's like her. It was ... quite a shock seeing him staring at me like that. I thought for a second ...'

He stopped. She looked up at him quickly, then looked away again.

It's kind of tough for him, she thought. He must be feeling so strange.

'You were right, honey,' he said. 'I should have had your faith. I was so afraid that we wouldn't find anyone and you would end up miserably disappointed, or that if we did it might be even worse and there'd be some ghastly horror story. It's been a nightmare for so many Ethiopians these last twenty years.' He paused. 'And we don't know yet – I mean, we've only met Seyoum. We don't know what happened to everyone else in the family.'

Ahead, Kassa and Tom had reached the gate of the enclosure. Tom turned and called out, 'I can see it! The Land Rover with Ethiopian Airlines written on the side! It's come!'

Afra's joy evaporated at once and a cold dread seized her. For the last half hour she'd forgotten the rabid dog and her enemy the virus, that even now might be beginning to poison her body, but the realization of it came back with full force. Rabies didn't seem far-fetched or unbelievable any more. It was frighteningly real, horribly close.

I couldn't *bear* it, she thought. Not now, when I've just found them.

She could see the Land Rover now. A group of *faranji* tourists were climbing out of it, pulling their bags and rucksacks out from the back. In the middle of them she could just make out, in the near darkness, the smart khaki uniform of the Ethiopian Airlines official. He was looking harrassed, and the tourists were bombarding him with questions.

Afra wanted to hang back, afraid of the worst. Prof and Kassa had started to carve their way towards the uniformed official through the crowd. The doors of the Land Rover were already shut and the driver was back in his seat, ready to drive off. She saw the official look up at Prof and shake his head, clearly irritated at being so impatiently interrupted.

No! Afra was screaming silently inside her head. No, it's impossible! No!

The man jerked his head unwillingly towards the Land Rover, which was already pulling away up the dusty track. She watched, her heart thumping, as Prof, followed by Kassa and Tom, sprinted after it. Tom reached it first, but though he shouted the driver didn't seem to hear. Prof, overtaking him in a tremendous spurt of speed, gave the minibus a hefty whack on the side with the flat of his hand. The driver pulled up short and his furious face appeared at the window.

Prof went up to him, spreading his hands out placatingly and explaining in his halting Amharic. The man's face softened and as Afra watched, he reached over to the seat beside him, pulled out a medical thermos and put it into Prof's hands.

Afra felt the blood begin to flow back into her numb arms and legs and she bolted forwards to join Prof.

'Is that it?'

The thermos was small and insignificant. It was hard to believe that it held something that would save her life.

Prof was still talking to the driver. They had lapsed into rudimentary English.

'You take now, for the daughter,' the man was saying. 'Tomorrow you pay at Ethiopian Airlines office.' He saw Afra and broke into a smile. 'Aiee! You are too lucky! Five minutes before plane is taking off only, medicine comes to airport.'

He put in the clutch and drove off.

'Oh wow,' said Tom, and even in the near darkness Afra could see that under his freckles his face was scarlet with exertion. 'I thought we'd lost him. Yeah, and I thought you were a goner, too.'

'And me,' said Afra. 'I thought, That's it.' She was still shaky but her spirits were beginning to revive, like bubbles whizzing up inside a coke bottle. 'I know what you were thinking. You thought I was going to go crazy and run around dribbling and biting everyone.'

She stopped. She'd wanted to sound funny but her words had brought back too painfully the memory of the rabid dog and the moment when the stone had crushed its poor demented brain.

Prof was talking to Kassa. He was holding the precious package in both hands as if he was afraid it would fly away.

'So there's someone at the tourist hotel who's

qualified to give injections? You're sure of that, Kassa? That's excellent. Can you take us there right away?'

Half an hour later, Afra and Tom were perching on the edges of two large comfortable chairs in the foyer of the hotel. Afra felt scruffy and out of place. The foyer was full of noisy foreign tourists and smartly dressed hotel clerks. Prof had disappeared as soon as they arrived, in search of the medical auxiliary who could administer injections. The precious thermos containing the vaccine and the antibiotics lay on the table beside them.

Afra was feeling daunted.

'Hey, Tom,' she said in a low voice. 'What do you think they'll think of me?'

Tom was staring, fascinated, at a *faranji* who was festooned with so many cameras and camcorders that he clinked as he walked.

'Who?' he said, not turning his head. 'What are you talking about?'

'My Ethiopian family. How do I know they're going to like me?'

He turned to look at her, puzzled.

'Why shouldn't they like you? There's nothing wrong with you or anything.'

Afra said nothing.

'I mean,' said Tom, afraid he'd said the wrong thing, 'they'll be really pleased, I expect. They'll be over the moon. Bound to be. I would be, anyway, if a long-lost cousin or niece or grand-daughter or something turned up out of the blue. It would be like a miracle or something. Just amazing.'

Afra still said nothing.

'When I said there's nothing wrong with you,' said Tom, anxious to get it right, 'what I really meant was that – you know – there's nothing wrong with you. You're great. They'll be proud of you. I would be, anyway.'

'Thanks, Tom,' said Afra in a stronger voice.

He'd made her feel better.

At least he's honest, she thought. You can trust Tom. He says what he thinks.

'You're only a pain when you get carried away on a mission or something,' Tom went on. 'Just don't go storming in there telling them they've got to let the budgie go because it's cruel to keep him in a cage, or it's time they cleaned out the goldfish bowl, or took a bit more care of the rats they've got running around in the roof, or something.'

Afra giggled.

'They don't have budgies and goldfish here, dumbo. Anyway, that's so unfair. I never did anything like that.'

'Yes, you did.'

'No, I didn't. When?'

'Loads of times. I'll try and remember some if

you like, and I'll tell you in front of all your new family and then you'll get really embarrassed.'

He paused.

'Actually,' he went on, 'I've been sort of wondering too. I mean it's OK for you, because it's your family and everything, but what about me? I'm a bit spare now, aren't I? Maybe I'd better just go back and hang around with Kassa. I don't want to be in the way when you go and see them.'

She felt a bit guilty. She hadn't considered how Tom might be feeling. She thought about what he'd said.

'No,' she said at last. 'I really want you to come too. I mean you're family, sort off.'

'I'm not. We're just mates.'

'I know, but . . .' She was finding it hard to put into words. 'You belong to my other life. My American half.'

'I don't. I'm English.'

'OK, then my Nairobi life. It's so weird being split in two like this. I mean, the Ethiopian bit's kind of scary now it's real. Maybe it'll all go wrong or something. I just need a friend with me – someone I really know – who knows me. Please, Tom. I guess I need you right now.'

He wriggled in his seat, looking pleased.

'OK. I'll come. Look, here come Prof and the medical guy. It looks like they're going to pump the stuff into you at last.'

17

THE END OF THE QUEST

It was quite a long way to Afra's grandmother's house. Kassa was waiting for them when they left the tourist hotel, and he and Tom walked on ahead, chatting happily, while Afra and Prof followed them in silence, each absorbed in their own thoughts.

Afra had never felt so nervous in her life. Her palms were clammy and her skin tingled all over.

Kassa led the way up a steep incline and stopped outside a sturdy stick fence. He called out a question to a little boy who was standing beside the door of the tin-roofed house which stood square in the centre of the compound. The door was open, and light streamed from it. The little boy seemed too overcome to answer. He dashed into the house, calling as he went.

At once Seyoum came rushing out, and two or three younger people appeared in the doorway behind him.

'Welcome! Come in!' he called out, and even in the dark of the courtyard Afra could see that he was beaming with pleasure and excitement. 'My mother is waiting for you.'

He pushed Afra ahead of him in through the door. She was momentarily dazzled by the neon strip light overhead, and she looked round, her heart thumping, for an old woman who might be her grandmother. But the only people she saw were two shy teenage girls, a middle-aged man and a woman about Prof's age who had been sitting on two low sofas set at right angles in the corner of the room. The little boy had disappeared again.

'She is preparing herself. She is coming,' said Seyoum. 'Look, Afra, here is your family. This is your Uncle Fassil, and your Aunt Meseret.'

'My mother had another brother?' said Afra, confused.

'No. I am her only brother,' Seyoum said. 'Cousins, they are cousins.' He waved towards the two girls. 'And these are your cousins also, Rahel and Hirut.'

The girls giggled shyly and smiled at Afra. Everyone came up one by one to embrace her, and looked sympathetically at her bandaged hand. She was dazed. She hadn't expected all these people. They seemed unbearably foreign and strange.

She was dimly aware of Prof behind her, talking to Seyoum, and that Tom and Kassa had been invited in and were sitting down on a bench near the door, but her eyes were fixed on a curtain hanging across a doorway at the back of the room, next to an iron bedstead in the far corner.

She'll come out through there, I know she will, she thought.

The two young cousins saw her looking at the curtain and murmured sympathetically. One of them softly patted her good arm, and said, in broken English, 'She is coming. She is very happy.'

The curtain twitched back. An old woman stood there. She was tall and magnificent. Her head was bound in a black turban, and a *shamma* of the finest white cotton was draped around her shoulders and fell in elegant folds over her full white muslin dress. Afra's eyes were riveted on her face, on the long proud nose and the deeply shadowed eyes. The old woman's mouth was twisted, her chest heaving.

Then she opened her arms, and Afra walked into their embrace.

She stood still, her face pressed against the folds of white cloth, breathing in the faint smell of woodsmoke and spices and honey that clung to her grandmother's clothes, waiting for a wave of love and a sense of belonging to wash over her.

It didn't come. She felt empty.

The arms round her loosened. She looked up into the old lady's face, and saw that it was drawn and trembling with emotion.

'Hello, Granny,' she said shyly. 'I'm Afra.'

'Afra,' her grandmother repeated, and at the sound of her name, spoken so tenderly, a first ripple of warmth ran through Afra's veins.

The old woman tottered suddenly and Seyoum rushed forward. He guided her to the bed and helped her up onto it.

'It is her hip,' he said to Prof. 'It is painful for her. She cannot walk well now.'

The old lady settled herself cross-legged on the bed and beckoned to Afra, who perched gingerly on the edge of it, then, a little embarrassed, kicked off her shoes and took her place at her grandmother's side. A picture flashed into her mind of royalty, of a crown princess sitting beside an aged queen, and she tried to make her back as perfectly straight as her grandmother's.

Prof came forward now. He stood in front of his mother-in-law and bent his head right down as he took her hand in his. The breath caught in Afra's throat. She had never seen him show such respect to anyone before.

The old lady pulled her hand away and rested it on his shoulder. He raised his head and looked at her.

'*Inate*,' he said.

'He is saying "Mother",' Seyoum said quietly to her.

'*Lije*,' the old woman answered.

'She is calling him her son,' said Seyoum.

Prof stood up again and Afra could see that the eyes behind his glasses were welling over with tears. He tried to say something else in Amharic, but the words didn't come.

'She talked about you many, many times,' he said.

The old woman looked at him intently and shook her head, then she beckoned imperiously to Seyoum. Behind him Afra could see more people crowding into the room and a mass of curious faces peering in through the door.

'Sablay talked about her so much,' said Prof to Seyoum. 'Tell her.'

Seyoum translated rapidly. The old woman spoke again.

'She wants to know, did she suffer?' said Seyoum. 'Did she see her child?'

'Yes, yes,' said Prof. 'She saw her. She held her. She had no pain – just a terrible weakness, a great tiredness.'

Afra's own eyes were clouded with tears. She could hardly see him. She felt her grandmother's strong arm close round her and draw her closer. The old lady spoke again.

'You did not bring her to me until now, she says,' translated Seyoum. 'She heard the news of the child, and that Sablay had passed away. All these years she has longed for her.'

'I tried,' Prof said. 'I wrote. I sent messages, here, to Lalibela, and to Addis. I paid a radio station to broadcast a message to you.'

He had sat down now on the stool by the bed. He had taken his glasses off to wipe his eyes and hadn't put them on again. His face looked naked. Afra could hardly bear to see the sorrow in it.

Her grandmother was nodding and sighing.

'It is true,' said Seyoum. 'It was very hard for us, for so many years. Our land, all our property, was taken in the revolution. Then, after Sablay and I left, the government forces came to question my mother and she ran away and had to hide for so long, with cousins here and there. She was in the south, then in the west, then in Addis, and when I escaped from Ethiopia I was in this country and that country. Only five years ago she returned here back to her home, and only last year I came myself. No, you could not have found us.'

There was a little silence. Afra hardly heard the dishes clinking behind the curtain or the murmur of voices as Seyoum's words were translated into Amharic for the benefit of the onlookers.

The old woman turned suddenly towards her and, cupping a gentle hand under Afra's chin, looked down into her face.

'Sablay,' she murmured, tracing Afra's eyebrows with a forefinger.

She smiled, her whole face lighting up, showing a remnant of the beauty she must once have had, and spoke rapidly to Seyoum. He laughed and shook his head.

'What did she say?' asked Afra eagerly.

'She says she can see your mother in your eyes,' he said. 'But if . . .' He stopped and laughed again.

'Please,' she said. 'Tell me.'

'But if you are as . . . as . . . ' He was looking for the right words in English.

'Wild and headstrong,' said someone from the other end of the room. They all looked up. Giorgis had come in and was sitting with Uncle Fassil.

'She says if you're as wild and headstrong and full of mad impractical ideals as your beautiful mother was, heaven help your poor father. Or words to that effect.'

The tension snapped and bursts of laughter filled the room. Afra felt her grandmother's hand slip down to her shoulder. It rested there, shaking, as the old woman laughed and cried in turn, wiping her eyes on the corner of her *shamma* with her other hand. Afra began to laugh too, feeling her anxiety and numbness leach away and a kind of joy, a steady, rising tide of it, begin to fill her.

The curtain fluttered again and Aunt Meseret, with the two girls, came out. One was carrying a beautiful round table made of red basketwork, covered with a conical lid, and the others were bringing steaming dishes of spicy stew. They set them down in front of the bed. The crowd of onlookers began to melt tactfully away through the open door. Seyoum saw Tom and Kassa hovering uncertainly.

'Come!' he called to them. 'Eat with us.'

Chairs were brought forward until everyone in the family was seated round the basket.

'What are you doing here, Giorgis?' said Prof jovially. 'You're not family exactly.'

'My dear Richard,' said Giorgis placidly, holding his right hand out over the bowl which Rahel was offering to him, while she poured a stream of water over it from a jug so that he could wash it. 'I'm sure I'm related somehow. My grandmother came from Lalibela, you know, and everyone's a cousin of everyone else's round here. Anyway, Seyoum bumped into me down in the town and invited me.'

He moved his chair so he was sitting beside Prof. Aunt Meseret lifted the lid off the basket table with a flourish.

'Ah,' said Prof, looking at the huge pieces of fine *injera* lying in it. 'I'd forgotten how wonderful home-made Ethiopian food can be, and as for the hospitality—'

'Hospitality?' interrupted Seyoum. 'There is no need for hospitality. This is your family, Richard. You are in your own home.'

Prof stretched his legs out luxuriously, then, tucking them back under the stool, leaned forward to tear off a piece of *injera*.

'So I am,' he said.

Afra's grandmother had torn off a piece of *injera* too. She rolled a tender morsel of lamb in it, then turned to Afra and put the succulent bundle into Afra's open mouth as if she was feeding a small child.

Afra looked up at her. The old woman's face was already becoming familiar, her large eyes, her softly-pouched round cheeks, the high ridges of her brows.

I'm going to learn Amharic, Afra told herself. I really, really am. I've got to be able to talk to her myself, properly.

'I don't – speak – Amharic,' she said tentatively.

To her relief, her grandmother smiled.

'No – English – me,' she said.

On the far side of the table, Tom was sharing a bench with Kassa. Trickles of red juice were running down his chin and his face was pink and sweating. He caught Afra's eye.

'This stuff's hot, isn't it?' he said. 'Blows the roof of your mouth off. Nearly as bad as vindaloo.'

'You like it, though?' she mouthed back at him across the table. She felt defensive. She wanted him to like everything.

He grinned.

'It's great. But I'll have awful . . . well, you know, wind and everything tomorrow.'

She looked round nervously, hoping no one had understood. She wasn't sure if it was terrible manners to talk about wind in Ethiopia.

Luckily no one had noticed. Everyone was busy eating and talking. Seyoum, Prof and Giorgis had their heads together. They were discussing politics, of all things, as if any of that stuff mattered at a time like this. Hirut and Rahel, under the watchful eyes of Aunt Meseret, were doling out more chicken and lamb stew onto the *injera*.

A boy appeared at the door. He came in shyly, crossed the room to Uncle Fassil and greeted him quietly.

I've seen him before, Afra thought.

The boy looked up and at once she recognized him. He was the young deacon she'd seen that first morning in the church.

'This boy is my nephew, so he is also your cousin,' Uncle Fassil called out cheerfully. 'He is deacon.'

The boy smiled at Afra and slipped onto the bench beside Kassa. She felt triumphant but not surprised. She'd known at first glance, that morning in the church, that he was something to do with her. She opened her mouth again, like an obedient chick, for the mouthful that her grandmother was holding out for her. She didn't need to speak to the boy. She would save him up for the future, a future that now stretched so enticingly ahead.

Afra's grandmother changed position on the bed, grunting with pain, and Prof, looking up, saw the grimace on her face.

'What's wrong with her hip?' he asked Seyoum quietly.

'It is arthritis. It hurts her too much.'

'Has she seen a doctor?'

'Yes. I took her to Addis. The doctor tells me she must have an operation. But the surgeon there, I was not sure about him. Also I do not have the money. It is very expensive.'

'Is it?' said Prof. 'We'll have to see about that.'

Giorgis and Fassil were engaged in an energetic conversation. Giorgis turned a laughing face to Prof.

'Just as I thought, Richard. This fellow's uncle married my mother-in-law's first cousin. That means you and I are practically cousins too.'

Prof raised his eyes.

'Spare me,' he said. 'Fellow archaeologists is bad enough. When are you coming to Nairobi, anyway? There's so much we have to talk about.'

'I don't know. When are you going back?'

'Soon. Very soon. To Addis first. I have to get Afra to a proper doctor. She'll need a thorough check-up and another jab in a day or two. Oh, by the way, can you take animals on Ethiopian Airlines flights?'

'Animals?' Seyoum looked up, startled.

'Animals?' repeated Giorgis. 'What animals?'

'Only my little dog,' said Prof, holding his hands out to Rahel, who was waiting with the jug and bowl so that he could rinse them.

Tom and Afra's eyes met. Tom's face was bursting with laughter.

'*My* dog,' he mouthed.

Afra grinned back at him. She'd known all along that Prof would end up agreeing to keep Wusha. She needed time, though, to get used to the idea that he'd taken Wusha on as his own dog.

An image of the garden in Nairobi came vividly into her mind, with the ramshackle bungalow in the background, and Sarah in her yellow dress standing in the doorway, and Joseph feeding his goat handfuls of grass, and Stumpy the goose waddling towards her with fond raucous honks, and Kiksy the bushbaby flying through the air to land on her shoulder. It was great that Wusha was going to be there too, and just as well perhaps that Prof would be the one to look after him. Stumpy and Kiksy might be jealous otherwise.

It was strange thinking about Nairobi, here in this different world. She shut the images out again and looked around her.

Aunt Meseret had lit an oil lamp. The electric light had flickered and gone off now that the town's generator had shut down for the night. The lamp cast a soft glow on the circle of faces, highlighting everyone's coppery cheeks and lighting up the warm pools of their eyes.

She let her gaze linger on one after the other, on Uncle Seyoum, Fassil and Meseret, and her two young cousins; on Tom her old friend, and Kassa her new one; on Giorgis in his smart designer clothes and Prof in his shabby old ones. She was in the middle of them, alongside her very own grandmother, a person of solid flesh and blood, from whom she could feel strength and love radiating as warm and real as the light from the lamp.

This is my family, she thought. This is my place.

Outside in the darkness the mysterious churches of Lalibela lay silent in the moonlight, and beyond them were the mountain tops, the high places of Ethiopia.

Up there, on the plateau, was another rare and precious family, the last survivors of another ancient race. They too would be together now, huddling against each other, sharing their warmth against the freezing wind. And when the morning came, they would lift their heads and howl, and their wild haunting songs would echo across the land.

Elizabeth Laird
**Wild Things 1:
LEOPARD TRAIL**

AFRICA!

Tom Wilkinson, just arrived from England, finds his new
country an amazing place. Exotic birds call outside his
window. Monkeys clamber on the roof. A vast game park
stretches beyond the garden. And next door lives a strange
girl with a house full of orphaned animals.

But dangerous predators haunt the night. When a hungry
leopard moves into the neighbourhood, Tom and his new
friend Afra hatch a desperate plan to save the beautiful
creature from being shot . . .

Elizabeth Laird
Wild Things 2:
BABOON ROCK

Deep in the African bush! It'll be the best birthday of Afra's life.

Her present is a trip to Baboon Rock, living in the wild among elephants, cheetahs and zebra. Tom and Joseph are sharing the adventure and, best of all, her busy father is coming too.

But her dad breaks his promise. And Afra's disappointment makes her disobey all the rules. After dark, she creeps out alone, desperate to save an abandoned baby baboon. And herself becomes the prey of some hungry night hunters . . .

Elizabeth Laird
**Wild Things 3:
ELEPHANT THUNDER**

*'Elephants,' said the wildlife ranger, 'are the most dangerous
animals in Africa.'*

Tom has never seen an elephant in the wild. He's always
loved the massive, majestic beasts – and now Titus Musau is
taking him and Joseph to Mount Kenya to observe them at
close quarters. Despite the warnings, Tom can't wait to get
there.

But nothing could have prepared him for his first elephant
encounter. A young, wounded bull, screaming in pain and
rage, and charging straight for him!

WILD THINGS titles
available from Macmillan

The prices shown below are correct at the time of going to press. However, Macmillan Publishers reserve the right to show new retail prices on covers which may differ from those previously advertised.

ELIZABETH LAIRD

1. Leopard Trail	0 330 37148 7	£2.99
2. Baboon Rock	0 330 37149 5	£2.99
3. Elephant Thunder	0 330 37150 9	£2.99
4. Rhino Fire	0 330 37151 7	£2.99
5. Red Wolf	0 330 37152 5	£2.99
6. Zebra Storm	0 330 37153 3	£2.99

All Macmillan titles can be ordered at your local bookshop or are available by post from:

**Book Service by Post
PO Box 29, Douglas, Isle of Man IM99 1BQ**

Credit cards accepted. For details:
Telephone: 01624 675137
Fax: 01624 670923
E-mail: bookshop@enterprise.net

Free postage and packing in the UK.
Overseas customers: add £1 per book (paperback)
and £3 per book (hardback).